Luke Temple was born on Halloween, 1988. As a child, Luke didn't enjoy reading, he was terrible at spelling and found writing hard work. Yet today he's an author! When not writing, Luke spends most of his time visiting schools and bringing his stories to life with the children he meets.

Find out more at: **www.luketemple.co.uk**

Collect all the 'Ghost Island' series:

☐ Ghost Post

☐ Doorway To Danger

☑ The Ghost Lord Returns

Collect Luke's 'Felix Dashwood' series:

☐ The Traitor's Treasure

☐ The Mutating Mansion

☐ The Traitor's Revenge

Collect Luke's books for 5-7 year olds:

☐ Albert and the Blubber Monster

☐ Albert and the Giant Squid

THE GHOST LORD RETURNS

Dear Paige,

Luke

2018

LUKE TEMPLE

Gull Rock Publications

Dedicated to the Holy Well at Holywell Bay,
27 years in the finding!

With thanks to Jessica Chiba, Catherine Coe, Gareth Collinson,
Kieran Burling and Mike and Barbara Temple

www.luketemple.co.uk

Copyright © Luke Temple 2016
Cover and illustrations © Jessica Chiba 2016

First published in Great Britain by Gull Rock Publications

All rights reserved. Apart from any use permitted under UK copyright law, this publication may only be reproduced, stored or transmitted, in any form, or by any means, with prior permission in writing from the publisher or in case of reprographic production in accordance with the terms of licenses issued by the Copyright Licensing Agency and may not be otherwise circulated in any form of binding or cover other than that in which it is published and without a similar condition being imposed on the subsequent purchaser.

All characters in this publication are fictitious and any resemblance to real persons, living or dead, is purely coincidental.

The paper used in the printing of this book has been made from wood grown in managed, sustainable forests.

ISBN: 978-0-9572952-7-8

Printed and bound by CPI Group (UK) Ltd, Croydon, CR0 4YY

A catalogue record of this book is available from the British Library

1

The Woman and the Clowns

Have you ever seen a ghost?

Chances are that if you have lived on Thistlewick Island long enough, the answer to that question is yes. Throughout Thistlewick's dark and mysterious history, more ghosts have been spotted than Albert Gailsborough has caught fish or Filbert Morris has caught rats. That is a lot of ghosts!

Most of these supernatural beings are harmless, but some are rather harmful – from the ghost of a postmaster seeking revenge by cursing the post to the pirates whose ships sank off our shores.

One ghost that has never been seen, though, is that of Lord Thistlewick, the great man who created our island in the 18th century. People who have tried to find Lord Thistlewick's ghost have not only been unsuccessful, they have also met with a very unpleasant fate.

From *The Dark Side of Thistlewick Island* by Sandi Foot

The bright green and orange hair caught Becky's attention as she walked down Watersplash Lane. It sat on top of the heads of two clowns, both with big painted smiles, walking in the opposite direction.

If today hadn't been the start of the Thistlewick fair, that would have been weird, but Becky guessed they were part of the circus performance due to take place tonight.

As the clowns passed her, she saw a small, round woman waddling along behind them.

She was staring at her hand and muttering, 'How do I get this thing to work?'

Becky did a double take as she saw what the woman was holding: an EMF detector – a rectangular black box used to find ghosts.

Questions started buzzing in Becky's mind. Why did the woman want to find ghosts? Was she looking for a particular one, or just hunting in general?

Until that moment, Becky had thought she was the only person on Thistlewick Island interested in ghost hunting. She had used an EMF detector herself to find the ghost of an old postmaster, and an evil spectre.

The woman was now hitting the EMF detector against one of the clowns, hissing, 'Stupid, stupid thing!'

There was something about the sneering expression on her face that made Becky suspicious.

She turned around, deciding to follow the woman and clowns and see what they were up to.

She kept her distance as they strode past the coconut shy and merry-go-round on the island green, which was filled with younger children. At the edge of the green they turned right. They were heading towards the church.

Map of Thistlewick Island

From *The Dark Side of Thistlewick Island* by Sandi Foot

The woman looked around. Becky quickly turned away and pretended she was very interested in Mrs Turner's toffee apple stall. Out of the corner of her eye she saw the flash of orange and green slipping into the church graveyard.

Becky crept over to the tall hedge surrounding the graveyard and found a gap. She crawled into it and peeled back a branch. There was the woman, squeezing in between the gravestones, the clowns close behind. They reached the centre of the graveyard and stopped at a large rectangular tomb, far bigger than anything around it. The tomb of Lord Thistlewick.

The woman got out her EMF detector and waved it around the grey stone.

Why is she doing that? Becky wondered.

The tomb had nothing in it, everyone knew that. When Lord Thistlewick died his body was never found. The tomb was only symbolic – a reminder of the great man who created Thistlewick Island. Without a body there, his ghost wouldn't be hanging around the tomb.

The woman waved the EMF detector about again, looked at it, then threw it at the orange-haired clown.

She beckoned to the green-haired one. 'Bartley!'

He reached into the pocket of his baggy polka-dot trousers and pulled out a thin yellow pole. The pole kept growing and growing until it was the size of a walking stick, with a black circle at the end of it.

A metal detector, Becky realised.

The woman grabbed it from Bartley and moved it around the tomb.

So she's looking for a ghost and hunting for metal?

Whatever the woman was up to, it wasn't working.

'Gah!' She thrust the metal detector back to Bartley and stormed out of the graveyard.

Becky waited until they were a good distance up the lane before she followed again.

A group of workmen were coming the other way, carrying large pieces of circus tent. Becky had to step off the path to let them past, and briefly lost sight of the woman and clowns.

When the workmen had passed by, the mysterious trio had vanished. Becky hurried along the path, looking left and right, wondering where they had gone.

She walked around the corner of the island hall but quickly jumped back. The two clowns were standing outside, either side of the door, almost like they were guarding it.

Becky stayed hidden round the corner and watched. A minute later, the woman came out of the hall, followed by Mayor Merryweather, dressed in his grand purple robes.

'I am sorry that I cannot be of more help, Mrs Ramsbottom,' the mayor said. 'But Lord Thistlewick left no will on Thistlewick Island.'

Mrs Ramsbottom, Becky thought. *Who is she? And why is she so interested in Lord Thistlewick?*

'That's OK, Mayor. Thank you ever so much for your help.' She smiled sweetly at him.

'Well, I must be off to practise my speech. Will we see you later for the opening of the fair?'

'Oh, of course.'

Mayor Merryweather returned her smile, nodded to the two clowns, then strode away from the island hall.

As soon as he was gone, Mrs Ramsbottom's face turned to thunder. She glared at the clowns. 'Any more bright ideas, Barney?'

The orange-haired clown drew a circle in the air with his hand.

'The fortune teller.' Mrs Ramsbottom nodded, seeming to understand. 'Yes, perhaps the old supernatural art form is worth investigating. I saw her setting up in the market square earlier.'

Becky was determined to find out what Mrs Ramsbottom, Bartley and Barney were up to. She knew a short cut to the market square down an alley, so arrived there before them. The market square was crammed full of red-and-white-striped stalls and tents.

Becky spotted her mum at the other end, hair tied in a tight bun, setting up her cakes next to Mr Morris's splat-the-rat game. Becky hid between tents and watched the mysterious trio cut across the market towards Mrs

Didsbury's fortune-telling tent. Bartley, the green-haired clown, ripped the tent flap open. They all stepped inside.

Becky crept over and pressed herself to the side of the tent, trying not to breathe too loudly. The material was thin, so it was easy to hear through.

'I am sorry, the fair hasn't started yet. Would you mind coming back later?' came Mrs Didsbury's croaky voice.

'I'm afraid I am in a bit of a hurry,' said Mrs Ramsbottom. 'I wondered if you could tell me anything about Lord Thistlewick's ghost.'

'Oh… Who are you, may I ask?' asked Mrs Didsbury.

'Mrs Ramsbottom,' said Mrs Ramsbottom. 'Fortune tellers have a connection with the supernatural, do they not? So there must be something you can tell me?'

There was a pause, then Mrs Didsbury said, 'I am afraid it is not something I can discuss with just anyone.'

'So you do know something?'

There was another pause.

'You must tell me.' Mrs Ramsbottom's voice was now far from friendly. 'Tell. Me!'

'I am sorry…' Mrs Didsbury said.

'Bartley, Barney!' Mrs Ramsbottom snarled.

Chairs clattered and Mrs Didsbury gave a yelp. Becky stood frozen. She thought about helping Mrs Didsbury, but she didn't want to give herself away before finding out what Mrs Ramsbottom was up to.

'No! Don't! Please, stop!'

'Will you talk?' asked Mrs Ramsbottom.

'OK, OK! I will tell you,' Mrs Didsbury cried.

The tent went silent. Becky pressed her ear to it.

'All I know is that many years ago,' Mrs Didsbury whispered, her voice trembling, 'a fortune teller at the Thistlewick fair made a prophecy.'

'Go on,' snarled Mrs Ramsbottom.

'When the rock on Watcher's Cliff falls again, Lord Thistlewick will return and a true Thistlewickian will find his treasure.'

'I see… So if this rock is pushed, the true Thistlewickian gets the treasure?'

She's after Lord Thistlewick's treasure! Becky realised.

'I only know what the prophecy says,' Mrs Didsbury replied weakly.

'Fine,' said Mrs Ramsbottom. 'Now don't you go telling anyone about our little meeting here. I saw you out walking with four dogs earlier. Are they your pets? I would *hate* for anything bad to happen to them.'

Becky frowned. The woman was threatening Mrs Didsbury.

'Becky, what are you doing snooping around the tents?' She wheeled around. Mum was standing behind her, hands on hips. 'You could have been helping me with my cakes.'

'Sorry, Mum.'

'Anyway, everyone's heading over to the main tent for the opening of the fair. Come on!'

2

The Rock on Watcher's Cliff

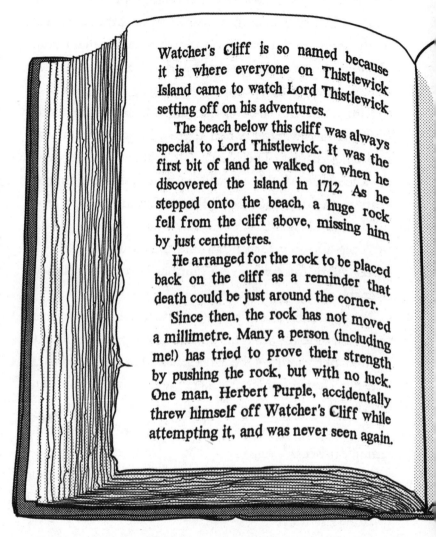

Watcher's Cliff is so named because it is where everyone on Thistlewick Island came to watch Lord Thistlewick setting off on his adventures.

The beach below this cliff was always special to Lord Thistlewick. It was the first bit of land he walked on when he discovered the island in 1712. As he stepped onto the beach, a huge rock fell from the cliff above, missing him by just centimetres.

He arranged for the rock to be placed back on the cliff as a reminder that death could be just around the corner.

Since then, the rock has not moved a millimetre. Many a person (including me!) has tried to prove their strength by pushing the rock, but with no luck. One man, Herbert Purple, accidentally threw himself off Watcher's Cliff while attempting it, and was never seen again.

From the award-winning book, *My Fascinating Life with Rocks*, by Rocco Hardcastle

'It is two o'clock on Friday, and that means that I can officially welcome you to the grand opening of the annual Thistlewick fair!' Mayor Merryweather boomed to the large crowd sitting on benches in the main tent. His twirly moustache glistened and, under the spotlight, Becky thought his purple robes made him look like a giant plum. 'As always, the fair will run from today until Sunday evening, when there will be a spectacular fireworks display. This year's fair marks a very special occasion. On Monday it will be exactly three hundred years to the day since Lord Thistlewick first discovered our beautiful island.'

A big 'Oooohhh' went around the crowd.

'To mark this, we have a number of events planned over the weekend...'

Becky looked to her right and saw Mrs Didsbury over the other side of the tent, hunched over and trembling. Behind her, right at the back, were Mrs Ramsbottom and her clowns, obviously keeping a close eye on her. Becky felt sorry for the old fortune teller.

'So they really threatened her?' Jimmy whispered, sitting on Becky's right.

Becky nodded. 'I think they're trying to find Lord Thistlewick's treasure.'

'Who are they?'

'They're definitely nothing to do with the circus performing at the fair,' said Finn, on Becky's left. 'I saw

10

them arriving at the harbour this morning. All those clowns have red wigs. That woman sounds dodgy.'

Becky looked back at the mayor as the crowd started laughing at something he had said.

When the laughter died down, Becky looked back at Mrs Ramsbottom again. But she wasn't there, and neither were her clowns. Becky scanned the tent and saw a circle of green disappearing through the exit. 'Where are they going?'

'Let's follow them and find out,' Finn suggested.

Becky and Finn stood up, but Jimmy stayed firmly in his seat. He was glancing at his mum, sitting next to Becky's mum and Finn's granddad.

'Come on, Jimmy,' Becky whispered. 'They won't notice. They're all too busy enjoying Mayor Merryweather's speech.'

As another laugh rang around the tent, he got up and they crept to the aisle, up the steps and out into the afternoon sun.

There was no sign of Mrs Ramsbottom or the clowns.

'I think I know where they've gone,' said Becky.

Finn looked at her blankly.

'Watcher's Cliff!' Jimmy realised. 'To make the prophecy come true.'

'Come on!' Becky hurried along the paths and lanes, Finn and Jimmy close behind, weaving in between the old cottages on the east of Thistlewick Island.

They eventually came to Greentree Lane. Becky put a finger to her lips and they crept up the steep lane. As they reached the top, Becky stopped. Watcher's Cliff was ahead of them and there, standing around a large slab of granite, were Mrs Ramsbottom and her clowns. The rock was just as tall as the woman, and almost as round.

Becky, Finn and Jimmy hid behind the corner of a cottage and peered out.

'She's using her EMF detector again,' Becky realised.

'What's the orange-haired clown waving about?' asked Finn.

'Barney? A metal detector,' said Becky, recognising the long yellow pole.

'They don't think Lord Thistlewick's treasure is actually *inside* the rock, do they?' asked Jimmy.

'I don't know what they're thinking,' said Becky.

With a yelp, Mrs Ramsbottom threw her EMF detector to the ground and started pushing against the rock. Her whole body wobbled with effort, but nothing happened.

Finn sniggered. 'She's trying to make the prophecy come true.'

'Don't just stand there, help me!' she yelled at the clowns.

They both stepped up to the rock and put their backs against it.

'Do you think we should stop them?' asked Becky.

'No!' said Finn, still grinning. 'There's no way they'll be able to get that rock to fall.'

He was right. All three of them pushed and pushed, but it didn't move a millimetre.

The woman stood back and kicked the rock.

'Stupid thing!' she spat, puffing heavily. 'We need machinery. We'll get this rock off the cliff if it takes seven bulldozers.'

Mrs Ramsbottom walked away, along the cliff edge, calling to the clowns, 'Come on!'

They looked at each other, then followed.

When they were out of sight, Becky darted into the open. 'Let's go and look at the rock.'

A gentle wind hit them as they moved towards the cliff edge.

Becky went up close to the rock. There was nothing special about it. Just a big slab of grey, like an overweight gravestone.

She ran her hand across the dull moss covering the rock, then turned to Jimmy and Finn and shrugged.

Jimmy's eyes widened. 'Becky, look out!'

A rumbling noise came from below her. Her feet started to shake. So did the rock. Cracks appeared in the ground around it, thin at first, but they grew wider and deeper. Becky ran backwards, staring at the cliff edge.

Soon, the part of the cliff on which the rock stood was completely separated from the rest of the cliff. Becky's eyes nearly popped out of her head as she watched the rock roll back and forth.

The ground under it crumbled and the lump of granite fell with lightning speed.

Thud!

Becky stood there, speechless. She heard a gasp and turned to see Mrs Didsbury on Greentree Lane, hovering by the end cottage. She had obviously decided to follow Mrs Ramsbottom as well.

'You pushed the rock... The rock fell... You are the true Thistlewickian.'

'I-I didn't p-push it. It just...' Becky stuttered.

But Mrs Didsbury wasn't listening. She was already hobbling back along the lane, towards the centre of Thistlewick.

Becky bit her lip. Mrs Didsbury was a big gossip. She couldn't talk about Mrs Ramsbottom, but there was nothing stopping her from telling everyone about the rock falling. Becky knew that soon everyone on the island would know about the prophecy, and think she was the true Thistlewickian.

'I really didn't push it,' she told Jimmy and Finn. 'I just ... stroked it.'

'Look, down there.' Jimmy pointed.

Becky thought he meant the fallen rock, until she looked over the newly created edge of the cliff. Seagulls soared past the golden sun, and below them was a boat.

Now it was Finn who gasped. 'Look what it's called.'

Becky squinted at the golden lettering on the side of the ship. '*The Caspian.*'

'That's the name of Lord Thistlewick's son,' Jimmy realised. 'You think that's Lord Thistlewick's boat down there?'

Finn nodded slowly.

A shiver ran through Becky as Jimmy said, 'So has Lord Thistlewick actually returned? Is the prophecy really coming true?'

Becky turned to Finn.

'Can we go out in a boat – without your granddad knowing?'

Finn grinned. 'Sure, I can manage that. Why?'

'We're going to go and investigate *The Caspian.*'

'Tonight?'

'Tonight!'

3

The Caspian

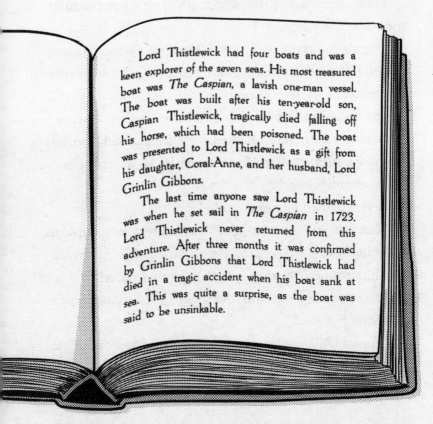

Lord Thistlewick had four boats and was a keen explorer of the seven seas. His most treasured boat was *The Caspian*, a lavish one-man vessel. The boat was built after his ten-year-old son, Caspian Thistlewick, tragically died falling off his horse, which had been poisoned. The boat was presented to Lord Thistlewick as a gift from his daughter, Coral-Anne, and her husband, Lord Grinlin Gibbons.

The last time anyone saw Lord Thistlewick was when he set sail in *The Caspian* in 1723. Lord Thistlewick never returned from this adventure. After three months it was confirmed by Grinlin Gibbons that Lord Thistlewick had died in a tragic accident when his boat sank at sea. This was quite a surprise, as the boat was said to be unsinkable.

From *Breaking Waves: Important Boats and Their Influential Owners*
by Bob Shipman

Becky shut herself in her bedroom for the rest of day. She had arranged to meet Jimmy and Finn by the harbour at eight o'clock. That was when the circus performance was due to start in the main tent. Normally, Becky would have loved to have seen the circus, but she had to convince Mum that she couldn't go. She was pretending to be ill.

She lay on her bed under the low, slanted roof, thinking about the fallen rock. She went over and over the moment in her mind. Mrs Ramsbottom and the clowns had put all of their weight into pushing the rock, but Becky had barely touched it. Why had it fallen? It must have been a freak of nature.

Her mind turned to the prophecy. Perhaps it really was coming true and they would find Lord Thistlewick on *The Caspian*. For this to happen, she had to hope that Finn could get a boat for them without his granddad noticing.

Becky's bedroom, in the flat above the Thistlewick post office, looked out over the market square. When the fair started up at four o'clock, the chatter from the people in the square drifted up to where she lay.

'Has Seraphina Didsbury told you?'

'Did I hear mention of a prophecy?'

'Yes! Apparently Lord Thistlewick is going to return to the island and give someone his treasure!'

'Why?'

'Because a rock has fallen!'

'How?'

'It was Becky Evans!'

'I heard she pushed it herself…'

'Seraphina said that it means Becky is the true Thistlewickian.'

'When will Lord Thistlewick return?'

'Will he give Becky Evans his treasure?'

Becky remembered that part of the prophecy: '... *and a true Thistlewickian will find his treasure.*' Maybe when she, Jimmy and Finn went to investigate *The Caspian* they would find Lord Thistlewick *and* his treasure. She couldn't stop the excitement tingling in her stomach.

At seven thirty, Mum popped her head round Becky's door.

'I hear that you're the true Thistlewickian. It's all people have been talking to me about today. They keep asking how you managed to push that rock.'

'I didn't push it – it just fell,' Becky said quickly.

'I know, you told me,' said Mum. 'But people will gossip. Anyway, it's time for the circus.'

'Mum, I'm not feeling great. I don't think I should go.'

'You missing the circus? You must be ill!' Mum sat down next to Becky on the bed and felt her head. 'You are a bit hot, love. Staying here is probably for the best, rather than having old Mrs Didsbury badgering you. I'll leave you to get some rest.'

Becky nodded. 'I can come to the circus another day.'

***

Becky stared at the rowing boat floating in the harbour. It had no sail – just two seaweed-covered planks to sit on and a couple of oars to row with. The boat looked like it had once been painted yellow, but now it was the dull colour of rotten wood.

'Is this the best you could find, Finn?' Becky asked.

'I can't take Granddad's main fishing boat – he'd be suspicious if he came back from the circus and it wasn't here.'

'But this one will sink as soon as a wave hits it!' Jimmy was staring at the two large holes in the side of the boat.

'No it won't. Granddad's had it since he was a kid. It's lasted this long for a reason. It's called *Patch*.'

Ignoring the holes, Becky breathed in the salty sea air. 'Let's do this!'

'I'll go in the front and navigate. You two can row,' Finn instructed.

Becky climbed into *Patch* and helped Jimmy gingerly over the side. The boat creaked and wobbled. Becky tightened the straps on her rucksack, so it wouldn't slip off her shoulders.

'What's in there?' asked Finn.

'Bottles, candles, an EMF detector…'

'Things for communicating with ghosts?' asked Jimmy.

Becky nodded. 'But just one ghost today. Lord Thistlewick.'

'Let's hope *The Caspian*'s still anchored off Watcher's Cliff then,' said Finn.

He undid the rope securing *Patch* to the harbour wall and jumped in. Becky and Jimmy took an oar each and with a last look behind them to check no one was watching, they set off.

Soon they were out in the open water. Waves crashed into the boat, making it groan ominously, shooting spray up into their faces.

'How do we get to Watcher's Cliff?' Becky called over the noise of the sea.

'It's not far,' said Finn. 'We head east, then follow the coast until we get to the really tall cliff with all the jagged rocks in front of it. That's Watcher's Cliff.'

Jimmy seemed to turn green at the mention of jagged rocks.

Even though it wasn't dark yet, the sky was grey with stormy clouds. The wind started to pick up as they rowed onwards and the ancient boat swayed heavily from side to side. Becky's arms began to ache – it was like rowing through treacle.

After ten minutes the harbour disappeared behind them under some thick, low-lying mist. This closed in around them, but Finn made sure they kept the edge of Thistlewick Island in sight all the time.

'We'll need to be careful in a minute,' called Finn. 'Those jagged rocks are coming up.'

Becky saw the rocks in front of them, like a herd of sharks' fins waiting to attack. If *Patch* hit one, it would sink faster than the rock had fallen from the cliff.

They successfully navigated in between the first two razor-sharp rocks.

Becky saw a large silhouette floating in the mist ahead. '*The Caspian*'s still there!'

'You need to take your oar out of the water, Becky,' Finn ordered.

She did so and, with only Jimmy rowing on his side, *Patch* swung left, just missing another rock.

'Wow, look at it! What a boat!' Finn called back, pointing to the silhouette, which was growing larger by the second.

'There's another rock at twelve o'clock,' said Becky.

Finn looked back at her. 'What?'

Becky gritted her teeth as the wind howled into her. 'Rock straight ahead!'

'Huh?'

Both Becky and Jimmy shouted now. 'We're going to hit a—'

'Rock!' Finn finally realised. 'Row, Jimmy, row!'

It was too late. *Patch* wouldn't swing far enough. The rock was centimetres away, lots of sharp points sticking out of it like a bed of nails.

'Push against the rock, Finn!' Becky called. 'Push us away from it.'

He leant over the side and Becky grabbed hold of him so he didn't fall in. Jimmy kept battling against the waves with his oar. Finn pressed his hands against the rock and groaned as he pushed it.

It seemed to work. At the last minute *Patch* pulled left and they just missed the rock. Finn's hand was cut slightly, but he didn't show any pain.

Just as Becky breathed a sigh of relief there was a loud *CRACK!* and the boat shook.

'Oh no,' Jimmy mouthed.

Becky looked down and saw water seeping in between her feet.

'The rock must be bigger under the water,' said Finn. 'It's split the wood!'

Panic ran across Jimmy's face.

'Row, both of you. Straight ahead, fast as you can!' yelled Finn.

Becky plunged her oar into the water. It was a race now – could they get to *The Caspian* before the sea swallowed them up?

The water between them and Lord Thistlewick's boat seemed clear of rocks now, but the waves tossed them about and cold water flooded around their feet.

Weighed down by the water, the back end of *Patch* started to sink into the sea. Jimmy jumped to the front and it tipped back up again.

'Nearly there!' shouted Finn, leaning out towards *The Caspian*. He grabbed on to something and began pulling himself up.

Through the mist, Becky saw Finn dangling from a rope attached to *The Caspian*.

With his free hand, Finn reached to his side and grabbed another rope. He swung it towards Becky. She caught the end of it and held it out to Jimmy.

He frowned at it, unsure what to do.

'Grab onto it and Finn will pull you up.'

Jimmy lifted a shaking hand and gripped the rope tightly.

Finn sent another rope down for Becky. Without thinking, she grabbed it and swung out of the sinking *Patch*. Her feet bounced against the hard wood of *The Caspian* and she started to pull herself up it.

As Finn was helping Jimmy, Becky made it to the top first. She grabbed hold of the railings and lifted herself up and over and onto the deck.

Looking around, she saw it was empty, with just the mist swirling around it.

'Give us a hand,' came Finn's voice.

Becky glanced over the side of the boat. She held out her hand to meet Finn's, and saw *Patch* being swallowed up by the angry sea below.

Finn collapsed onto the deck while Becky helped a trembling Jimmy over the side.

'How are we going to get back to the harbour now?' asked Jimmy.

'We can think about that later,' said Becky. 'We're on *The Caspian*!'

Two huge masts stretched up into the mist. At the back half of the boat was the main cabin, marked out by colourful stained-glass windows, with the boat's giant wheel on the raised deck above.

Finn ran his hand along the polished wood railing. 'It's in amazing condition for a boat built in the eighteenth century. I thought it sank when Lord Thistlewick died.'

Jimmy shrugged. 'No one knows exactly what happened.'

'We can ask him when we find him,' said Becky, taking her EMF detector out of her rucksack.

'I reckon it's a fake,' said Finn. 'I've seen shipwrecked boats before. It's in too good a condition to have been underwater.'

'It's the real thing all right,' came a woman's voice, making them all jump.

Becky turned and saw a round figure stepping out of the main cabin – Mrs Ramsbottom.

The two clowns stepped out from behind her.

Becky frowned. 'What are you doing on here?'

The woman's mouth spread into an ugly grin. 'I could ask you the same thing. What are you doing on *my* boat?'

4

Godiva Gibbons

> The two living members of the Thistlewick family who are most closely related to Lord Thistlewick are Steven and Godiva Gibbons. They are direct descendants of Lord Thistlewick's daughter, Coral-Anne, and her husband, Grinlin Gibbons. Steven briefly came to Thistlewick Island to film a ghost hunting TV show earlier this year, but Godiva has never travelled to the island. She is largely a mystery; we only know that she has owned several large construction companies in England.

From *The Thistlewick Family: An Intimate Biography*
(300th Anniversary Edition) by Sandi Foot

'This isn't your boat,' said Becky. 'This is *The Caspian*, Lord Thistlewick's boat.'

Mrs Ramsbottom shook her head.

'I told you it's a fake,' Finn muttered.

'And I told you it is real.' The woman glared at him. 'It *used* to belong to Lord Thistlewick, but now it belongs to me. Call it my inheritance.'

'So you're related to Lord Thistlewick?' asked Becky.

Jimmy gasped. 'You're not Mrs Ramsbottom. You're Godiva Gibbons.'

The woman turned to him. 'Yes,' she snapped. 'And you must be Jimmy Cole. My brother told me about you. He said you were smart.' She looked at Becky. 'And that makes you Becky Evans.'

Becky frowned. 'What do you mean, your brother?'

'He likes playing with ghosts and has a bad taste in clothes…'

'Spooky Steve?!' Becky cried.

Spooky Steve was the reason the post office ghost had turned up, when Becky and Jimmy had had their first supernatural adventure. He had turned out to be a nice enough person, but Becky definitely wasn't sure about his sister, especially with the two clowns leering behind her.

Jimmy and Finn moved in close to Becky, as if they felt unsafe too.

'Why are you trying to find Lord Thistlewick's treasure?' Becky asked.

Godiva frowned. 'How do you know I am?'

'I heard you threatening Mrs Didsbury earlier.'

'I knew someone was spying on me.' Godiva spun around to the clowns and spat, 'You should have spotted her!'

The clowns stood there motionless, their painted expressions stuck on happy.

'I know about the prophecy,' said Becky.

'Then you'll know what the rock falling off Watcher's

Cliff means. If you were following me, did you see it happen? How did it fall?'

'I didn't see,' Becky lied. 'I only saw you trying.'

'Well, anyway, it doesn't matter who pushed it. The prophecy says the rock needed to fall, but it doesn't say that the true Thistlewickian needed to push it themselves. When Lord Thistlewick returns I will have his treasure.'

'What makes you think you're the true Thistlewickian?' asked Finn.

'Weren't you listening?' Godiva pulled a long face at him, like he was stupid. 'I'm Lord Thistlewick's descendant.'

'So is Spooky Steve,' said Becky.

Godiva sighed. 'My weak brother seems to think that the treasure belongs to this island, not to us Gibbons.'

'And he's right,' said Finn. 'If Lord Thistlewick has left any treasure around here, it belongs to all of us, not just you.'

'You've never even been to Thistlewick Island before!' said Becky.

Godiva's face was starting to glow red, and her voice grew high with anger. 'That treasure should have gone to my ancestor, Grinlin Gibbons, but Lord Thistlewick was too greedy to let him have it. Instead, it's somewhere on this island. Maybe you've all been hiding it for him. Now I have returned, as the true Thistlewickian, to take what I deserve.'

Becky folded her arms. 'We're not going to let you.'

'Oh, and how are planning to stop me?'

'We'll tell everyone on the island what you're up to,' said Finn.

Godiva's expression changed to a frog-like grin. 'Good luck with that. Bartley! Barney!'

As one, the two clowns stepped forwards, arms outstretched.

Becky clenched her fists and prepared for a fight but, before she could do anything, Finn let out a loud scream and charged between Becky and Jimmy.

He started kicking the shins of Barney, the orange-haired clown, but Bartley quickly grabbed Finn by the neck and pulled him away.

Becky ran up and yanked hold of the clown's arms. He was stronger than he looked and threw her to the ground with a single shake.

Becky looked up and saw the creepy painted mouths of Barney and Bartley smiling down at her.

'Jimmy, do something!' she cried, but Jimmy was frozen with fear.

Barney grasped hold of Becky's hair with his left hand and Finn's with his right, and began dragging them along the deck.

'Aaarrrghhh!' Becky cried through gritted teeth.

***

29

'Why did you have to go and kick them?' asked Jimmy.

'They would have locked us up anyway,' Finn replied shortly.

They were squashed together in a small, empty store-cupboard on *The Caspian*, with one of the clowns – Bartley, the green-haired one – the other side of the door. The only light was the dim beam that stretched through the small metal bars at the top of the door.

Finn reached up to the bars and tried tugging on them, but the door didn't budge.

Bartley glared in, his red nose pressing against the bars.

'How long are you going to keep us here?' asked Finn.

The clown's painted smile widened. He grunted and walked away.

'OK,' Becky whispered. 'I've got an idea. Jimmy, it's time for you to meet someone very special, who me and Finn know well.'

Jimmy frowned while Finn looked puzzled.

'Willow,' Becky said under her breath.

'Oh!' Finn nodded.

Becky continued, 'You said I should call for you when I needed help. Well, I need help now. Willow, can you hear me?'

They waited. Nothing happened.

'What now?' asked Finn.

'We keep waiting, I guess.'

Another few minutes passed, and Becky started to wonder whether the ghost girl would come.

'It's getting chilly in here,' said Finn.

Jimmy looked at Becky. 'Ghosts need energy to show themselves, don't they?'

'And they get it by sucking up heat.' Becky glanced around excitedly. 'I think Willow is coming.'

A small silver speck darted in front of Becky's eyes. It became a ball of silver light, floating in the middle of the cupboard. The light exploded like a small firework and spread over a human shape, revealing the floating, see-through image of a girl with golden hair and a long, flowing dress.

'Hello, Becky,' the ghost girl said softly. 'And Finn is here too! It is wonderful to see you both again.'

'It's amazing to see you too, Willow!' Becky grinned. 'This is Jimmy.'

Willow smiled at him. 'Hello, Jimmy.'

He clung tightly to Becky's arm, his eyes wide. She remembered that he had only seen one ghost before: the old postmaster, Walter Anion, who had been quite scary.

'It's OK, Jimmy, Willow is the nicest person I've ever met, living or dead.'

Jimmy continued to stare at the ghost girl nervously.

'How are you, Willow?' asked Becky.

'I am well. But how have you three ended up trapped in here?'

Becky told her about Godiva Gibbons and the prophecy.

'She certainly sounds unpleasant,' said Willow.

'I reckon she's evil,' said Finn.

'Just like her ancestor, Grinlin,' said Becky.

Willow cocked her head curiously. 'And what made Grinlin Gibbons evil?'

'We found out about him when we met the ghost of Walter Anion. Grinlin framed Walter for the murder of Lord Thistlewick's son.' Jimmy explained.

'But it was actually Grinlin who did it,' Becky added.

Willow raised her eyebrows. 'Wow. That is evil.'

'We need your help, Willow,' said Becky. 'We have to escape from this boat. The clown outside locked us in this cupboard. Do you think you could get the key from him?'

'I will give it a go. I am not very good at the whole spooky ghost thing, but I will see if I can somehow scare him off. That way, he won't see you escaping.'

With another smile, Willow disappeared from sight.

5

Godiva's Deal

People often think that all ghosts are scary. Of course, many ghosts are rather terrifying, but only because they came from people who were just as terrifying when they were alive.

The ghosts of good people, on the other hand, have no desire to scare the living, and you should not be afraid of them.

From *My Life With Ghosts* by Eric Pockle,
published after the author's death

When Willow appeared again she was giggling.

'I didn't need to spook the clown. He is fast asleep on a chair.' She held a small metal key out in her pale hand. 'I got this. You can sneak right past him.'

'Thank you, Willow!' Becky beamed and took the key.

She inserted it into the store cupboard door. It turned and the door creaked open. They all crept out quietly.

The only exit was a small hatch in the ceiling with stairs leading up to it, right next to where Bartley was slumped in the chair. His big red nose vibrated as he snored.

They shuffled past him, Finn stifling a laugh, and trod lightly up the stairs to avoid the wooden boards creaking. Soon they were up on deck. Willow floated close by.

There was barely any light left in the sky now – just a silvery haze from the crescent moon. Becky guessed it had to be after ten o'clock. She looked all around but couldn't see any sign of Godiva or Barney.

'Godiva will be somewhere around, so we need to be quiet,' Becky warned.

'How exactly can we escape?' whispered Jimmy. 'We don't have our own boat any more.'

Becky looked into the dark water below. It was completely different to earlier – flat and calm. 'We'll have to swim to shore and climb up the cliff.'

'I'm up for that,' said Finn.

Jimmy groaned. 'I don't have any choice, do I?'

They found the ropes they'd used earlier dangling from the boat and hoisted themselves over the railings. Becky was careful to tread lightly past the portholes down the side, in case Godiva and Barney were in the cabins.

Finn jumped into the water. 'It's actually not that cold.'

Becky leapt from the boat and splashed down next to him. He was right – the water was fine.

'Come on, Jimmy.'

Jimmy slowly shifted himself down the rope, trying not to look down into the water. He soon ran out of rope and fell, landing in the sea with a high-pitched squeal.

The three of them paddled through the still water, Willow's silvery glow lighting their way as she hovered above them towards the shore.

Becky felt a great sense of relief as her feet touched the soft sand. They had escaped from Godiva and her clowns! She shook the water from her arms and looked up at the huge expanse of Watcher's Cliff, silhouetted against the moonlit sky like a towering giant.

'It's tall, but there are loads of holes, so it should be easy to climb,' said Finn, shaking the water off himself. 'Even for Jimmy.'

'Oi!'

The two boys walked towards the cliff. But Becky's attention had been caught by something else – the fallen rock, sitting in a crater of sand to their left, the moonlight shining directly onto it. She walked over to it and frowned.

'What's the matter?' asked Willow, floating over to join her.

Becky placed her hands on the rock and pushed. She put all her weight into it, but it wouldn't budge. 'How *did* it fall?'

Willow shrugged. 'I don't know.'

Becky reached a hand up to the top of the rock. Unlike the other rough sides, it was flat and smooth.

'This must have been the bottom of the rock when it was sitting on the cliff.'

Her fingers made out indentations, like something was carved into it. She stood on tiptoes and made out delicate, old-fashioned letters.

'*If success is to find you, start by proving an unlikely rumour true.*' Becky looked at Willow. 'What does that mean?'

But Willow didn't answer. She hurriedly fizzled out of sight.

'Don't move, or the boy gets it!'

Becky felt the water soaking her clothes turn to ice. She wheeled round to find where the voice had come from. She saw Finn, frozen a few metres up the cliff, staring to his right. Becky followed his gaze. Godiva walked out from under the shadow of the cliff with Barney, who was holding Jimmy. Jimmy tried to kick out, but the clown was too strong.

Godiva pursed her lips. 'I've always wanted to say something like that.'

'Let Jimmy go!' yelled Becky, angry at herself for not keeping an eye out.

Godiva ignored her. 'You really are a problem, aren't you? What am I going to do with you? I can see there's no point in trying to lock you up again.' Godiva walked up to the rock. 'No. Instead, I will make you do the work for me. You can find Lord Thistlewick's treasure and save me the effort.'

Becky thought fast. Had Willow fled, or was she still with them, just invisible? Maybe she could scare Godiva.

'Willow?' Becky whispered, but there was no response.

'Whatever it is you have to say, girl, you can say it to me.' Godiva's eyes fired into her.

Becky tried not to panic and looked to Finn for help.

'Our parents will be wondering where we are,' he said, his face tense.

'With the Thistlewick fair on? They'll just think you're out playing on the merry-go-round, or whatever children do these days.'

'I told my mum where we were going,' Becky lied. 'She'll come looking soon. Then you'll be in trouble for kidnapping us!'

Godiva stared at Becky long and hard.

'I don't believe you. You wouldn't have told your parents you were coming here. They wouldn't let you.'

Just then, Becky heard a faint sound from above them. Godiva looked up in surprise.

A voice called from the top of Watcher's Cliff, 'Becky, are you down there? I am here with Finn and Jimmy's parents. We are all worried about you.'

Becky breathed a sigh of relief. 'See, told you my mum would come looking.'

Godiva's mouth fell open and she ran back into the shadow at the bottom of the cliff while the clown dragged Jimmy there.

'Becky? Can you hear me?' the voice came again.

'If you know what's good for you, do not reply,' Godiva hissed.

Becky walked over to the cliff. 'Let us go, and I won't call up to her.'

Godiva hesitated for a moment.

'Becky?' the voice called down.

'If we don't go home soon, my granddad will be coming here in a boat to find us,' said Finn.

'Fine,' said Godiva. 'But you're finding that treasure for me.'

Becky nearly laughed. 'Why would we do that?'

Godiva moved so close that Becky's lungs were filled with her sickly perfume. 'Because if you don't, I can see a different prophecy coming true.' Her voice changed into a scary sing-song one, like she was reading an evil nursery rhyme. 'If Becky Evans does not bring Lord Thistlewick's treasure to Godiva Gibbons by the end of the fair, then Godiva will demolish all the buildings on this island, one by one, until she has found his treasure.'

Finn looked like he wanted to punch something. 'That's not a prophecy, that's a threat.'

'You couldn't do it!' cried Jimmy. 'You wouldn't be allowed to knock buildings down.'

'Thistlewick Island still belongs to my family. I can do what I want with it.' Godiva's eyes flared darkly. 'So, you will find Lord Thistlewick's treasure?'

Becky gritted her teeth – she didn't have any choice. 'Yes.'

'Off you go then.'

The clown let Jimmy go. Becky walked past Godiva, not meeting her gaze, and joined him. They gripped onto the bottom of the cliff, ready to climb.

'Oh, and don't try any tricks – I'll be watching your every move,' Godiva added. 'If you dare tell *anyone* about our deal, I'll make sure the first building I knock down is your mum's post office!'

Her mouth spread into another frog-like grin.

***

The three children trudged back home along the coastal path. Becky felt worn out from the evening's events.

Finn puffed out his cheeks. 'Is she really allowed to destroy Thistlewick if she wants to?'

'Not sure,' Jimmy replied. 'We can ask Mayor Merry-weather if her family still owns Thistlewick Island.'

'But would she really destroy the island her ancestor created?' asked Finn.

'I don't think Godiva Gibbons has much Thistlewick blood in her. She's far more like Grinlin Gibbons. If he murdered someone to get what he wanted, I'm sure Godiva will do anything,' Becky said grimly.

They turned right onto Watersplash Lane and Becky

heard people chattering as they walked out of the main tent – the circus must have just finished. A few people came down the lane towards them.

Becky shot behind a nearby bush.

'What are you doing?' asked Finn, stopping beside her.

'Hiding. Everyone thinks I'm the true Thistlewickian. I don't feel like being asked about that now.'

'But according to Godiva, *she* is the true Thistle-wickian,' Jimmy pointed out.

'You don't actually believe that, do you?' said Finn.

Jimmy shook his head.

A fourth person appeared next to Becky. Jimmy jumped back.

'Willow!' Becky grinned. 'You saved us from that evil woman – thank you.'

'I knew it was Willow pretending to be your mum!' said Finn.

The ghost girl smiled. 'It is what I am here for – to help you.'

'So what are we going to do now?' asked Jimmy.

'The prophecy says that Lord Thistlewick will return, so we need to find him – and before Sunday evening. There's no way he'll let Godiva take his treasure.'

'And he outranks her,' said Finn. 'Godiva won't be able to destroy Thistlewick if he is here.'

'But Lord Thistlewick died over two hundred and

fifty years ago and his ghost has never been seen on Thistlewick. How are we meant to find him in two days?' asked Jimmy.

'I don't know,' Becky admitted. 'But there was writing on the bottom of the rock. It must be a clue.'

Willow nodded. '*If success is to find you, start by proving an unlikely rumour true.*'

'An unlikely rumour?' asked Finn.

Jimmy's eyebrows creased together in thought. 'It must be an unlikely rumour about Lord Thistlewick.'

'And if we prove it true, maybe we will find his ghost,' said Becky.

'I'm taking part in a Scrabble competition at the library tomorrow morning. I'll do some research while I'm there,' said Jimmy.

Finn screwed up his face. 'Scrabble competition? Really?'

'Godiva said we can't tell anyone what we're up to, so we have to act normally,' said Jimmy. 'My mum's entered me into the competition.'

'I will talk to some other ghosts and see if they know of any rumours about Lord Thistlewick,' said Willow.

'I can ask Granddad,' said Finn. 'He knows a load of stories about the island.'

'And I will go and see Mayor Merryweather and ask if the Gibbons family really can do what they want on this island,' said Becky.

She peeked out from behind the bush. Watersplash Lane was empty now.

'I'd better get home before Mum does. Let's all meet up tomorrow after Jimmy's Scrabble competition and see what we've found out.'

6

Lord Thistlewick's Beard

'The Thistlewick Beard Appreciation Society is formed on the belief that Lord Thistlewick once had a beard. We hold a number of events each year to celebrate facial hair. The highlight of our busy events calendar is the Beard Competition, held as part of the annual Thistlewick fair.

'People often ask me for proof that Lord Thistlewick had a beard. While I know this to be a fact, our society aims to find actual evidence for our claims. It is true that no written record mentions Lord Thistlewick having had facial hair, and we have not yet found a painting of Lord Thistlewick with even the remotest sign of stubble. However, I live in hope that one day we will find the evidence to silence our many doubters!'

Ginger-Ann Curly, president of the
Thistlewick Beard Appreciation Society

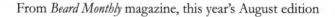

From *Beard Monthly* magazine, this year's August edition

Becky stepped out of the island hall feeling grumpy. She looked at her watch: 11.45. She needed to walk quickly to get to the library and meet the others.

She kept her head down as she passed islanders on

Watersplash Lane. She didn't want them asking her questions about being the true Thistlewickian.

Maybe she should enjoy the fact that everyone thought she was. But it just didn't feel right. Not when Godiva Gibbons was threatening to destroy the island.

Becky found Finn waiting outside the library, hands in pockets, but she couldn't bring herself to smile at him.

'What's got you in a bad mood?' he asked.

'The Gibbons family do own most of Thistlewick,' Becky explained. 'We sort of rent the island from them. Mayor Merryweather said it's like the Queen of England – she has the power to declare war on other countries and things like that, but she never does. It's the same on the island – the Thistlewick and Gibbons families have always just left everyone here to get on with our lives.'

'But Godiva does have the power to destroy Thistle-wick?' asked Finn.

Becky nodded. 'She can do what she wants. What did your granddad say?'

'Since Mrs Didsbury told him about the prophecy, that's all he's been interested in talking about. He kept asking me how you pushed the rock. I had to help him clean up the harbour hut in case Lord Thistlewick shows up there.'

'But he didn't know about any rumours?'

'Nope.'

'I haven't seen Willow yet. Maybe she's managed to

find something out from the other ghosts,' said Becky.

'I have,' came a voice.

'Aaahhh!' Finn cried.

Becky laughed when she saw the pair of blue eyes floating in front of him.

The rest of Willow seemed to grow out from the eyes, and she was floating beside Finn. It was like she'd been waiting to appear.

'Sorry,' said Willow. 'I just wanted to practise being spooky.'

'It worked!' said Finn, running a hand through his hair.

'What did you find out, Willow?' asked Becky.

'There are a few rumours, but none of them seem useful. One rumour is that Lord Thistlewick was allergic to cats, but I met a ghost who sold him four kittens.'

'Oh…'

'However, many of the ghosts told me something very interesting. There is a reason no one has ever met Lord Thistlewick's ghost.' Becky found herself leaning in curiously as Willow continued, 'When he died, Lord Thistlewick arranged for his ghost to be bottled.'

'Wow!' said Becky. 'You'd have to be brave to do that.'

Willow nodded. 'It is the most painful thing that can happen to a ghost. All your particles squished together in a bottle. Worse than death, some say.'

'So we have to find a bottle?' asked Finn.

'I guess so,' said Becky.

Willow disappeared from sight as the library door opened.

Becky heard her whisper, 'I shouldn't let myself be seen by other living people. I will carry on asking around the ghost world.'

A dozen or so people filed out of the library, Jimmy at the back of them.

'How did you do?' asked Becky.

He shrugged. 'I was beaten in the semi-final by a tourist from China.'

Becky patted her friend on the shoulder.

'There's always next year. I'll just have to study my dictionary harder.'

'Willow was telling us that Lord Thistlewick's ghost is in a bottle,' Finn explained.

'We still don't know what the unlikely rumour is, though,' said Becky.

'Well, I couldn't find anything in the books about Lord Thistlewick, but I did find this in the library's magazine rack.'

Jimmy held out a magazine. A man's face was on the cover, with a gigantic, fluffy beard. Above him were the words 'Beard Monthly'.

'There's an interview in here with Ginger-Ann Curly.' He opened the magazine to a page with a photo of a small, elderly woman on it.

'And she is?' asked Finn.

'The founder of the Thistlewick Beard Appreciation Society, and one of the only people to believe that Lord Thistlewick once had a beard.'

'But he didn't,' said Becky. 'At least not in any of the paintings I've seen.'

'Exactly. Most people think it's complete nonsense. That sounds like an unlikely rumour to me.'

'Me too!' said Becky.

'And look.' Jimmy pointed at an advert towards the bottom of the page. 'There's a Beard Competition at the Thistlewick fair this weekend. We can talk to Ginger-Ann Curly there.'

***

The competition looked like it was well under way when they slipped in through the entrance of the small tent.

'Now to our main contest, the beard that looks most like Lord Thistlewick's!' came the shrill voice of the small lady sitting on the front bench – Ginger-Ann Curly.

Becky, Jimmy and Finn crept over to a half-empty bench at the back.

'If there's no proof that Lord Thistlewick had a beard, how does she know what it looked like?' Finn whispered.

'It's whatever Ginger-Ann thinks,' said Jimmy. 'According to the interview, she used to think he had a ducktail beard. Now she believes it was a golden goatee.'

The first contestant stepped through a pair of red curtains, a long grey beard drooping down from his face.

'Nowhere near. Next!' Ginger-Ann ordered.

The grey-bearded man slunk off and a short, round man stepped through the curtains.

'I am The Beard,' he said in a comically deep voice.

It was an appropriate name. His big black beard covered up most of his face.

'Hmmm.' Ginger-Ann peered closely at The Beard. 'That looks suspiciously like…'

She stood up and stepped towards The Beard. The man backed away, but Ginger-Ann grabbed hold of his beard.

'Horsehair!' she exclaimed and yanked the beard. With a *ping*, it came clean off, revealing the red face of a woman.

Ginger-Ann sighed. 'Next!'

The curtains flicked open and the third contestant stepped out.

This man had completely missed the point of the competition – he didn't have a beard at all.

'Unless my sight deceives me, you do not have a beard,' said Ginger-Ann.

'That is correct,' the man replied.

'But, my dear fellow, this is the contest to find the beard most like Lord Thistlewick's.'

'Exactly. Lord Thistlewick didn't have a beard. I should win the competition!'

Ginger-Ann puffed out her chest. 'You ought to be careful what you say! I think you'll find that Lord Thistlewick had a golden goatee.'

'Prove it!' the man fired back at her.

'Get out of this tent, now!' Ginger-Ann screamed.

The next man seemed to have the same idea, though. Not only did he not have a beard, he was completely bald. After he was thrown out of the tent, another two men lacking facial hair appeared, and it turned out they were all part of a protest group, who thought the Thistlewick Beard Appreciation Society was a load of old rubbish.

Red faced and flustered, Mrs Curly said they would take a break before the next contest.

While the small crowd chattered to each other, Becky signalled to Jimmy and Finn and they moved to join Ginger-Ann at the front.

The old lady looked up. 'What do you want?'

'We read your interview in *Beard Monthly*,' Becky explained.

Ginger-Ann narrowed her eyes. 'And I expect you're here to tell me I'm wrong – that Lord Thistlewick never sprouted a single facial hair?'

'No, actually, we believe you.'

Finn screwed up his nose and raised an eyebrow.

Becky wasn't exactly telling the truth, but she needed to convince Ginger-Ann to talk.

It seemed to work – her eyes lit up. 'Well, it is a pleasure to meet you, children. In fact, you are Becky Evans, aren't you? The true Thistlewickian Seraphina Didsbury has been speaking of. Does that mean you have seen Lord Thistlewick?'

'No, Mrs Curly, not yet,' Becky said in a flat tone. She was getting bored of people asking her.

'Well let me know when you do. If I can meet the man himself, that will give me all the proof I need.'

'Mrs Curly,' Jimmy began, 'in your interview you said that Lord Thistlewick only had a beard *before* he came to Thistlewick. Why did he shave it off?'

'Ah, well, it took me many years of research to figure it out. Lord Thistlewick lost his beard in a near-death experience.'

How Lord Thistlewick nearly died
(according to Ginger-Ann Curly)

It was Lord Thistlewick's first proper adventure, years before he discovered our island. He set off from England, dressed in grand purple clothing, with a fine golden goatee, to find new land.

Soon he came across an island that was not on the map and met a local tribe that went by the name of Skegg. He tried to buy wood carvings from the tribe, so that he

could take them back home as proof of the island's existence. But the people of Skegg were not interested in his gold. They would only take payment in the form of hair, and were particularly interested in Lord Thistlewick's beard.

He was immensely fond of his beard and refused. The tribe became angry. They took him to a tree and tied him to a branch ... by his beard. All they gave him to escape was a razor-sharp blade.

That was painful enough, but then vultures arrived. Lord Thistlewick had a choice. He could either be pecked to death, or free himself from the tree by cutting his

beard off. After he was pecked a hundred times, he knew that his beard had to go.

After that terrible near-death experience, Lord Thistlewick never grew a beard again...

'But alas,' Ginger-Ann concluded, 'until I find proof, most people refuse to believe me.'

Becky looked to Jimmy, deep in thought, and Finn, who was pulling a sarcastic face as if to say, 'I'm not surprised.'

She turned back to the old lady. 'We'll help you find proof.'

'That is very kind, Becky, but I have spent sixty years trying without luck.'

'Have you found no clues at all?' asked Jimmy.

'No – if only I could get into his room at the White Wing Pub. It was once Lord Thistlewick's bedroom, and it is rumoured that it contains trophies and records of all his adventures. No one has been able to gain access to the room for hundreds of years.' Ginger-Ann sighed. 'I'm sure proof of his adventure to Skegg Island is inside, but the pub landlady, Ms Galway, won't even let me try.'

7

Words and Numbers

'When Lord Thistlewick died, his house was left unused for many years. Eventually tourism on the island increased and, in 1938, it was agreed that the house could be turned into a pub and hotel. The building work was overseen by Alfred Mosher Butts, an architect who also, famously, created the game of Scrabble.

The White Wing Pub and Hotel, as it is now known, is a beautiful place, with stunning views out to sea.

There is one room in the building that no one has been able to enter since it became a hotel: Lord Thistlewick's old bedroom. One man, Herbert Purple, tried to cut the door down with a chainsaw, but the chainsaw just bounced off. It narrowly avoided cutting Herbert's head off, but gave him a very fine haircut.

To this day, we do not really know what exactly is in Lord Thistlewick's bedroom.

From *The Thistlewick Family: An Intimate Biography*
(300th Anniversary Edition) by Sandi Foot

Becky strode along the coastal path towards the pub, Finn and Jimmy following.

'I know we have to prove an unlikely rumour true,' said Finn. 'But this is just *too* unlikely. Ginger-Ann's story was mad.'

'There's one way to find out,' said Becky as they arrived at the pub. 'Finn, can you distract Ms Galway? Me and Jimmy will see if we can find Lord Thistlewick's bedroom.'

The pub was buzzing with chatter as they entered. Islanders and tourists were settling down for afternoon meals and drinks.

'Finn, over here!' came a warm voice.

'Hi, Granddad,' Finn called back. He winked at Becky and Jimmy and went to join Albert in the corner.

Everyone stared at Becky, but she was getting used to ignoring it. She ducked her head, grabbed Jimmy's hand and quickly pulled him past the comfy chairs and tables.

'You're on the second floor, in the third room numbered four,' Ms Galway was telling a tourist when they reached the bar.

The tourist frowned. 'You have three room fours?'

Ms Galway smiled. 'It's one of the many quirks of this place. The numbering of the rooms on the second floor has always been random. There are six rooms and three are numbered four. No one knows why. The man who turned this place into a pub and hotel also created the game of Scrabble. I reckon he numbered the doors like that as sort of game that no one knows how to play.'

The tourist nodded uncertainly and Ms Galway offered to show him to his room.

Becky looked over to Finn, sitting next to Albert, who was talking enthusiastically to a bored-looking tourist. Finn nodded to Becky, and when Ms Galway appeared behind the bar again, Finn 'accidentally' knocked his granddad's drink off the table. It fell to the floor and smashed, and everyone around the pub turned to look.

'Sorry,' said Finn. 'My arm just slipped.'

'You're a clumsy one, aren't you?' said Albert.

Ms Galway bustled over to them with a mop. 'Not to worry. We'll have it cleaned up in a jiffy.'

Becky snuck quietly behind the bar and through the doorway at the back. Jimmy was looking around anxiously. She waved at him to hurry up and he scurried after her.

They climbed up a steep flight of stairs and found themselves on a landing with lots of identical doors leading off it.

'Any idea which is Lord Thistlewick's bedroom?' asked Becky.

'We'll know when we see it,' said Jimmy. 'It won't be any old door. It'll be special.'

They carried on up another flight of stairs and onto a second landing.

'All the doors look the same here too, apart from the numbers on them. This is the floor with three room fours, isn't it?'

'Look – the door at the end.' Jimmy pointed.

They walked up to it. Becky stared at the patterned frame made of rich, dark oak. At the centre was a finely-carved letter T, but no room number.

'This must be it. Ginger-Ann said no one's been able to get into the room, but there must be a way.'

'I've heard about doors that open when you knock on them in the right rhythm,' Becky suggested. She started tapping on the door.

'No, it must have something to do with this dial,' said Jimmy.

Becky looked at the metal box he was pointing at, to the side of the door. On it, there was a circular, golden dial surrounded by the letters of the alphabet in old-fashioned writing.

Jimmy leaned close to study it. 'There's an arrow. You can twist the dial so that the arrow lines up with different letters. The code to get into the room must be a word.'

'A word should be easy to figure out,' said Becky.

'Do you have any idea how many words there are in English?'

Becky remebered the ginormous dictionary Jimmy had at home. 'OK, lots. So let's start with the obvious words connected to Lord Thistlewick.'

'It's not going to be obvious, though. No one's been able to figure out how to get into Lord Thistlewick's bedroom for centuries.'

'OK, brainbox, over to you. What words can you think of that have something to do with Lord Thistlewick, but aren't obvious.'

Jimmy stared at the dial, a look of complete concentration on his face. Becky stood there, clicking her fingers impatiently.

'I really can't think of anything that no one else could guess.'

'But you've read all the books, Jimmy. You know everything there is to know about Lord Thistlewick.'

'I haven't read *all* the books – there are a lot of them. But even if I had, it's not going to be something from a book, otherwise anyone could look it up.'

'What about a name? Lord Thistlewick's son's name? His great-great-great-uncle? One of his four kittens?'

'Well, everyone thinks his great-great uncle was called Eva,' said Jimmy. 'But actually, he had a Scottish name that sounds like Eva but is spelt in a weird way: I O M H A R.'

'Try that, Jimmy!'

He slowly turned the dial to each letter.

'Come on, quickly. We don't want to be found up here.'

Jimmy turned the arrow to the final letter, ℛ.

Becky stared at the dial. Nothing happened.

She tried pushing the door. It didn't budge.

'This will never work,' said Jimmy. 'It could be anything.'

'What if we ask someone who actually knew Lord Thistlewick?' asked Becky, an idea forming.

'How?'

'Willow,' said Becky. 'She lives in the ghost world, and there will be ghosts on Thistlewick from Lord Thistlewick's time.'

'Good idea!' said Jimmy. 'She could ask them for likely words.'

'Willow, we need your help,' Becky called.

She tapped her fingers impatiently for thirty seconds, wondering how long they could stay up here without Ms Galway finding them. There was no sign of the ghost girl.

'Willow? Are you there?'

Willow's ghostly face appeared in front of the door, followed by a body.

'Sorry, I was at the other end of the island,' she said. 'I have been asking around about Lord Thistlewick.' She turned to Jimmy. 'You really don't need to look so worried, Jimmy, you've seen me appear before.'

'I'm not worried. It's just, you're flickering.'

It was true – her image was going in and out of focus.

'Oh.' Willow blushed. 'I guess it's the ghost equivalent

of being out of breath. How can I help you?'

'We need a word connected to Lord Thistlewick that's really unusual – that no one would be able to guess,' Becky explained.

'I know just the person I can ask,' said Willow. 'Lord Fairfield, who was at school with Lord Thistlewick, and owned Half Acre Farm in North Thistlewick. His ghost still haunts the cowshed there – I was talking to him earlier. I will be as quick as I can, but it might take me a while to get there and back.'

Willow faded from sight. Becky glanced down the hallway to check there was no one coming, then sat down on the floor next to Jimmy to wait.

It turned out that 'a while' for Willow meant a minute, because she quickly appeared again, flickering even more.

'Lord Fairfield was busy milking a cow.'

'He's a ghost. How did he manage that?' asked Jimmy.

Willow smiled. 'It was a ghost cow. Anyway, I was able to get one word out of him: McLardy.'

'McLardy?' Becky asked.

'It was the nickname Lord Thistlewick's friends gave him at school.'

'Perfect. Try it, Jimmy.'

He moved the dial around. Becky's excitement grew as he turned the arrow from letter to letter. She had a good feeling about 'McLardy'.

Jimmy reached the final Y. He waited, and…

'Nothing.'

'Oh…' Becky sighed.

'Back to the drawing board,' said Willow. 'Leave it with me. There are many more ghosts who I can ask.'

Just as she vanished, Becky heard a noise from the stairway. She walked back along the landing and heard footsteps coming up the stairs.

She peered over the banister and saw Ms Galway's head two flights below – she was obviously showing another tourist to their room. Why hadn't Finn stopped them coming up?

'Jimmy, Ms Galway's coming,' she whispered sharply. 'We need to get out.'

'How? The only way out is back down the stairs.'

Becky looked down again. There was a circle of bright green following the landlady up.

'It's Bartley!'

She looked around. There were lots of guest bedrooms. Maybe they could hide in one of them.

She ran over and tried tugging on a door, then another. Neither opened.

Ms Galway's voice echoed up the stairs. 'You will be in room ten, Mr … sorry, what did you say your name was?'

There was a long silence.

'I'll … er … just call you Mr Clown then. You must

be working with the circus. I saw it last night – really good fun. I thought you all had red wigs, though?'

'He must have been following us. We can't let him see us here. Think, Jimmy, think!' Becky hissed.

'I-I…' he stuttered.

Becky looked desperately at the doors and their numbers: 1, 4, 10, 4, 2, 4. It really was weird having the rooms numbered like that. Then she had a brainwave.

'Numbers and letters … Scrabble!' she exclaimed a bit too loudly.

'What?' asked Jimmy, glancing anxiously at the stairs.

'Ms Galway said the man who turned this into a pub also created Scrabble. What if the numbers on the doors are like numbers on Scrabble tiles?'

'Becky, you're a genius!' Jimmy did a little jump. He ran over to look at the doors.

Becky glanced back to the stairs – Ms Galway's voice was getting louder. She was asking Bartley what make-up he used to paint his smile on. There was, of course, no reply.

'Quick, Jimmy!'

'Argh!' Jimmy clenched his fists. 'It still might be impossible to work out. Ten is a helpful number – it only links to the letters q and z. But four is more common. It links to f, h, v, w … and y…' Jimmy's eye's lit up. 'Got it!'

He ran back over to the dial and Becky followed. She watched him turn it to different letters.

S.

Becky breathed in deeply.

Y.

She crossed her fingers.

Z.

Whatever the word Jimmy had thought off, she prayed it was right.

Y.

G.

Y.

Jimmy stepped back.

Becky frowned. 'Syzygy?'

'Yep!'

A mechanical whirring sound started. The dial sprang out of the metal box, which opened up to reveal a key on a hook.

Becky pumped a fist in the air. She grabbed the key and plunged it into the keyhole of the door.

As Ms Galway asked, 'Is someone up here? Hello? Can I help you?' Becky and Jimmy fell into the room and slammed the door shut.

8

The Room of Purple and Gold

SYZYGY

I love the word 'syzygy' because of its strange spelling. The fact that there are no vowels in it often catches people out. However, unless you are interested in astronomy, the meaning of 'syzygy' may be confusing.

Here is what it means: 'Conjunction and opposition of two heavenly bodies, or either of the points at which these take place, especially in the case of the moon with the sun.'

(Told you it was confusing!)

From *A Dictionary of the Weird and Wonderful* by Stephen Pelling

A purple haze surrounded them.

Ahead was a tall window made out of stained-glass diamonds in different shades of purple. As the sun broke through a cloud, its rays hit the window and highlighted the purple haze in gold.

'Purple and gold, Lord Thistlewick's two favourite colours,' said Jimmy.

Becky locked the door from the inside. 'What does syzygy mean? How did you guess that?!'

'I read it in my dictionary ages ago. Can't remember what it means, but it's such a weird word I didn't forget it – and it's the only one that works with those Scrabble numbers.'

Becky listened closely to what was going on in the corridor outside. She heard a door closing somewhere nearby and footsteps walking away down the stairs.

'Do you think the clown was following us?' asked Jimmy.

Becky nodded. 'Godiva said she was going to keep an eye on us. She doesn't trusts us, and I don't trust her.'

The sun's rays grew stronger through the stained-glass window, revealing the different parts of the room. The main feature was a grand, eight-poster bed; thick purple curtains hung from it with gold tassels. Some people said Lord Thistlewick was well over two metres tall and the bed was certainly the longest Becky had seen. It could belong to a giant!

On the wall behind the bed hung a huge variety of objects – swords, spears, horns, creepy face masks and even a stuffed boar's head.

'Those must be from some of Lord Thistlewick's adventures,' she realised. 'Maybe Ginger-Ann's proof will be in here.'

'I think you're right! Look at that painting.' Jimmy sounded excited.

She turned to face the wall opposite the bed and

above a stone fireplace was a painting of a powerful man with a thick, golden beard.

She gasped. 'That's Lord Thistlewick, isn't it?'

Jimmy read the inscription. 'Yes! It was painted in 1701, eleven years before he discovered this island.'

'So it's true,' Becky said in awe. 'Lord Thistlewick did once have a beard.'

'Ginger-Ann was right about the colour too – his beard was golden. Although it isn't a goatee, it's a proper beard.'

Becky had seen lots of images of Lord Thistlewick before, but never one quite so … she searched for the right word, and settled on … majestic. His figure, draped in robes (purple, of course) filled the whole canvas, and his dark eyes stared out, strong yet kind.

'We've done it, Jimmy. We've proved an unlikely rumour true!'

'And now success will find us. Does that mean the bottle containing Lord Thistlewick's ghost is in this room?'

'It must be. No one's been in here for centuries.'

Jimmy continued to look around the room. 'I can't see any bottles.'

Becky shook her head. 'It won't just be left out somewhere. That'd be too obvious. It'll be hidden.'

Becky glanced back at the painting above the fireplace. Lord Thistlewick looked out at her.

An idea flashed through her mind. 'Help me lift the painting down.'

'You think the bottle's hidden behind it?'

'Maybe.'

They took a side each and carefully lifted the painting away from the wall. They staggered under its weight but managed to carry it over to the bed and rest it against one of the posts.

Jimmy returned to the wall and felt along the part where the painting had hung. 'There's nothing here.'

'No loose bricks or anything like that?' Becky asked.

He shook his head. 'I suppose there could be a clue in the painting.'

Becky studied the painting closely, to see if she could spot any clues in it. It just seemed like a normal painting, with no hidden codes or unusual shapes that might tell them something.

Then she realised, 'The beard's been stuck on!'

She felt along the edge of the beard and dug a fingernail under it.

'What are you doing?' Jimmy tugged on her arm, trying to stop her.

The beard started to peel off Lord Thistlewick's face.

'Look, Jimmy!'

At the centre of Lord Thistlewick's newly revealed chin was a switch. Becky felt her heart beat faster as she flicked it. The bottom of the painting's frame fell off.

'Wow!' Jimmy mouthed.

Out of the gap in the frame rolled a small bottle with the longest, thinnest neck Becky had ever seen.

She carefully picked it up and took it to the window to see into it better. Something seemed to flicker inside the bottle – one minute it was there, the next it was gone. On the outside, pressed into the glass, was a large, golden letter T.

'This has to be it!'

'So … what do we do now?' Jimmy asked, staring at the bottle.

'We set Lord Thistlewick's ghost free!'

'And how do we do that?'

'Ghosts need energy. I guess he'll need a lot of it stuck in a bottle, so we need to heat the bottle up.'

'OK.' Jimmy went over to the wall of weapons and took something off it.

'A magnifying glass?' asked Becky.

'Hold the bottle up in the air.'

Becky did so, and Jimmy moved the magnifying glass around in front of it.

'What are you doing?'

'You'll see.'

The magnifying glass caught the light shining through the window and sent it shooting into the bottle.

Becky tried to hold the bottle still, but couldn't stop her left hand from shaking.

But no, it wasn't her hand shaking – it was the bottle. As the light continued to hit it, the bottle vibrated more and more until Becky's whole arm was shuddering with it.

'Shouldn't we take the cork out?' asked Jimmy.

Becky grabbed the cork with her right hand and pulled it from the top of the bottle. A sighing sound floated out of it. Becky held her breath – any second now, they would meet Lord Thistlewick!

The bottle stopped shaking. Becky didn't dare blink. The sun disappeared behind a cloud. Nothing happened.

Becky frowned. 'It didn't work.'

'Guuuhhh!' came a loud gasp from the bottle, making Becky nearly drop it.

A voice spoke now, deep and slow. *'Near death you found this bottle, but it is not as simple as you had hoped. My ghost was split, and here's a clue: there is a second bottle waiting for you!'*

***

'We heard Lord Thistlewick's voice.'

Outside the pub, Becky showed Finn and Willow the bottle, with the cork back in it. She told them what he had said.

'So Lord Thistlewick split his ghost into two bottles,' said Finn. 'That must be painful!'

'It would take a *very* brave ghost to do it,' Willow agreed.

'Where's the second bottle, then?' asked Finn.

'We looked everywhere in the bedroom and it's not there,' said Jimmy.

'Maybe it is connected to another rumour,' Willow suggested.

'Or to another of Lord Thistlewick's adventures,' said Becky.

'Not just his adventures,' Jimmy said slowly, thinking out loud. 'Lord Thistlewick said, "Near death you found this bottle". You found the first clue on the rock, Becky – the rock that fell and nearly killed Lord Thistlewick when he found this island – and Lord Thistlewick's beard nearly killed him too. So the second bottle might be connected to another near-death experience.'

'That makes sense,' said Finn.

Becky nodded. 'So to find the second bottle we need to find something else that almost killed him.'

***

Becky's bedroom was in darkness when she walked in. She let out a long sigh. They had spent the evening in the library, reading about Lord Thistlewick's many adventures. He hadn't faced death in any of them, so far.

She flicked the light on and her eyes widened. In the

middle of the floor was the model of her mum's post office she had created at school last year. But it was in ruins. Its roof had been smashed in and bits of it were spread across the carpet.

Becky bent closer and saw a note attached to the broken model.

It read: ONE DAY LEFT.

9

The Cursed Ship

Ships that have been wrecked off Thistlewick (G)

The Gannet – Date wreck found: 12th November 1980 –
Number dead: 15 – What happened?: seagull attack –
Coordinates: unknown

Gordon's Foot – Date wreck found: 23rd September 1900 –
Number dead: 1 – What happened?: capsized in a boat race –
Coordinates: Lat 50.93, Long −4.97

The Grimwood – Date wreck found: 3rd August 1720 –
Number dead: unknown – What happened?: unknown –
Coordinates: Lat 50.39, Long −5.15

Guppyboat – Date wreck found: 4th October 1988 –

From the Thistlewick Island Harbour Records

Becky woke to the ghostly vision of Willow floating above her bed, the moonlight highlighting her silver glow.

'Hello, Becky.'

'Willow! It's the middle of the night.'

'There is something I need to tell you.'

Becky sat up, suddenly awake. 'What is it?'

'I spoke to Mr Ziggy, who ran the fair when Lord Thistlewick was alive. He told me Lord Thistlewick

73

attended the fair every year except 1720, when he was ill in bed for a week.'

'What was wrong with him?' Becky asked, rubbing her eyes.

'Mr Ziggy doesn't know exactly, but he thinks it was something to do with a cursed ship.'

'Can you find out more?'

Willow nodded. 'I will try.'

Her figure fizzled out. Becky was alone once again.

Becky tried to get back to sleep, but she tossed and turned most of the night, impatient to find out more about the cursed ship.

By the morning, there was no sign of Willow, but Becky knew who she could ask. She jumped out of bed and looked out of the window. A storm was dancing overhead as the stall owners set up in the market. She found her waterproof and headed outside.

'It's Lord Thistlewick returning!' cried Mrs Didsbury, pointing to the sky.

Becky frowned. The prophecy said nothing about a storm. She pulled her hood over her head to avoid being noticed.

As the people in the market looked up, a bolt of lightning shot down.

'Aaaaahhhhh!'

The intense light blinded Becky for a moment. It started to clear and she blinked.

Gasps rang around the market as people pointed at a clump of scorched grass right at the centre.

'It is a sign,' Mrs Didsbury proclaimed loudly. 'Lord Thistlewick will be here soon.'

Becky rushed off, down Watersplash Lane. Ten minutes later, she was knocking on the harbour hut door. It creaked open and Albert peered out.

'Becky, come in, come in out of the rain.'

She saw Finn sitting in the corner, mending a fishing net. She took off her coat and sat down next to him, noticing that everything inside was unusually neat and tidy.

'One day soon I will open that door for Lord Thistlewick himself,' said Albert, joining them. 'Although I'm sure you will meet him first, as the true Thistlewickian. How did you push the rock? That is what I cannot imagine.'

'I didn't,' she replied flatly. 'And I'm not the true Thistlewickian, Albert.'

He smiled, seeming not to hear what Becky had just said. 'Well, bring Lord Thistlewick round when he arrives.'

'I wanted to ask you about a ship, Albert. A cursed ship.'

'There've been a few of those over the years.'

'This one had something to do with Lord Thistlewick becoming very ill.'

'Ah. *The Grimwood*,' Albert mouthed.

He glanced up at the wall opposite them. Becky followed his gaze and saw a glass frame hanging there. Behind the glass was something dark. She squinted and realised it was a piece of wood.

'Have I ever told you why that wood's behind glass?' asked the old fisherman.

Becky shook her head.

'I've heard *hundreds* of your stories, but that's one I've never heard either,' said Finn, surprised.

Albert leant towards them. 'That is the piece of wood that cursed Lord Thistlewick.'

How Lord Thistlewick nearly died

(according to Albert Gailsborough)

One night in 1720, just off Corkscrew Cliff, *The Grimwood* appeared.

A shipwreck floating in the sea, with no sign of any crew, living or dead. Surrounding the ship were thousands of dead fish.

The fishermen refused to go near the ship because of the effect it had had on the fish. Lord Thistlewick decided to investigate himself.

He rowed out to *The Grimwood* and carefully removed a small piece of wood, which he planned to show to a sorceress friend.

There was no sign of Lord Thistlewick for hours. Eventually the fishermen built up the courage to look for him. They found his rowing boat floating far out at sea. Inside, he was alive, but unconscious.

Lord Thistlewick lay seriously ill in bed for days.
His sorceress friend was given the wood to examine.
She found that a dark spell had been placed on it:
anyone who touched *The Grimwood's* wood would
be cursed.

The sorceress tried many spells and potions to cure Lord Thistlewick, but his condition worsened. He nearly died!

Eventually, as fireworks exploded to signal the end of the Thistlewick fair that year, the sorceess hit upon the right spell and Lord Thistlewick was saved from *The Grimwood's* curse.

Albert pointed back at the wood on the wall. 'That is the very piece of wood Lord Thistlewick took. It is kept behind glass, in case the curse still lives on in it.'

'Cool story, Granddad!' said Finn.

Albert nodded slowly. 'So when I meet Lord Thistlewick, I will ask him how it felt to be cursed. I have always wanted to know.'

Becky stared at the wood on the wall. Three words stood out from what Albert had said: *He nearly died!*

Thunder rumbled overhead and a splatter of rain hit the roof of the harbour hut.

'Doesn't look like it's clearing up out there, and it's too dangerous to fish in this weather.' Albert sighed. 'I shall head to the pub before the fair this afternoon. You two coming?'

Finn looked at Becky. She shook her head and whispered, 'Stay here.'

'The hut's getting a bit messy again, Granddad,' said

Finn. 'We'll stay and tidy it up. You never know, Lord Thistlewick might pay a visit later today.'

As soon as Albert had closed the door, Becky said, 'We have to find that ship. Lord Thistlewick nearly died because of it. The second bottle must have something to do with it.'

'Let's see if it's in the harbour records,' said Finn.

He went over to a small desk in the corner, opened a drawer and pulled out a huge red book.

'Good job we tidied up, or I'd never have been able to find this without asking Granddad.'

He laid it out on the desk. Becky came over.

'Most of the pages are just records of the numbers of fish caught,' said Finn, flicking through. 'Every day for hundreds of years. But I think if I turn to the back... Here we go, a list of all the shipwrecks.'

He kept turning the pages. The ships were listed in alphabetical order.

'There it is.' Becky pointed. '*The Grimwood*.'

'Wrecked on 3rd August 1720, and here are the coordinates.'

Finn handed Becky the book and she staggered under its weight. Finn walked over to the large fishermen's map of Thistlewick on the wall.

'I should be able to find it using the coordinates. What's the latitude?'

'Fifty point three nine,' Becky read from the book,

not really knowing what latitude was.

Finn ran a finger down the side of the map. 'And the longitude?'

'Minus five point one five.'

He moved his finger across the map and made an invisible circle with it. He stood back and stared at the map.

'I think I've found it. It's a hundred metres off the coast near Corkscrew Cliff. But how can we get there? We don't have Granddad's old boat any more.'

'Then we'll have to use his main one. You know how to sail it, right?'

Finn folded his arms.

'Come on, Finn, we have to find this bottle.'

He bit his lip and looked at the clock. 'OK. Granddad's usually in the pub for at least an hour. But in this weather it's not going to be easy.'

'Great! Do you have any diving equipment?'

'We're fishermen, not scuba divers. But there might be a snorkel in the cupboard over there. I'll get the boat ready while you look.'

***

'I can't see it. *The Grimwood* will have sunk right to the bottom,' said Finn.

Becky stared over the edge of the boat as it tossed

about in the angry waves. 'We have to see if the ship's down there.'

Finn frowned up at the darkening sky. 'It's too dangerous to dive down.'

'We haven't got time to worry. I'm going to take a look.'

She did up her waterproof and put on the goggles and snorkel she'd found.

'But, Becky…'

She leapt into the water, cutting off Finn's words. A wave quickly carried her away from the boat. Her heartbeat quickened, but she told herself to breathe normally as the cold water sloshed against her face.

'You're mad! Just be careful – and quick!' Finn called. 'We have to get Granddad's boat back before he notices, and I can't keep it here for long in this weather.'

Becky pressed her head under the water, but it was still too murky to see. She took a big gulp of air through the snorkel and dived under. She had been part of diving club at school last year. As the waves washed her from side to side, she remembered not to panic and kicked down deeper. Once she was away from the surface, the water became calmer – and a lot clearer.

There it is! She could see a shipwreck half-buried on the seabed a few metres below.

Becky had expected it to be surrounded by an eerie glow or something, but there was nothing to suggest the ship was cursed. She couldn't see any fish around it, though.

She spotted a hole ripped in the ship's side. Dare she swim through it? She knew she had to avoid touching the wood, but the hole looked big enough to avoid it.

The current swept Becky nearer. Pushing her hands through the water, she guided herself towards the hole until she was surrounded by dark wood.

Her heart thudded now. She only had enough air left for a quick look anyway. She moved carefully into the ship and found herself in what must have been the captain's cabin.

The walls were lined with bookshelves and maps, preserved by the water. A table stood at the centre, sand from the seabed eating into its legs.

A light caught Becky's attention. There was a gas lamp on the table – a *working* gas lamp.

How is that possible?

She glided towards it, careful not to touch anything made of wood. Next to the lamp was a bottle – small and round with a long thin neck.

That's it! Becky moved her hand through the water and grabbed it. She turned it and saw a large golden T marked in the glass.

Whoosh!

She spun round as a current of water blasted through the hole in the ship. There was nothing Becky could do

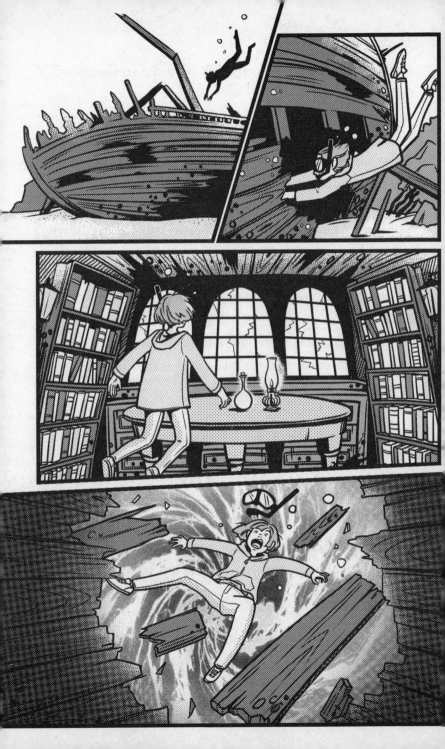

as the water picked her up and sent her crashing into the wall of the cabin. Her face hit the dark wood, sending her goggles and snorkel flying. The wood gave way and snapped with a dull ache, and the water carried her through to the other side.

The image of the outside of the ship swam in her eyes. She had touched the wood! Had it cursed her like Lord Thistlewick? She wanted to panic – her heart should be beating fast – but she couldn't feel a single heartbeat. Her body started to shake and a ball of fire shot up from her stomach to her throat. Her mouth opened and the last of the air escaped between her lips. Balls of fire soared along her arms and her legs, burning them and making them shudder wildly. Her eyes closed. She tried to shut out the pain but it was no good. The inside of her body was on fire!

She only sensed a little of what happened after that. A pair of arms wrapped around her body, lifting her up. Cold air hit her face, cooling some of the burning. Someone laid her down. Then her hand grew hot. But it was a different sort of heat – a pleasant feeling, which travelled from her hand to the rest of her body, putting out the fire and replacing it with a warm glow, like a mug of hot chocolate.

Becky opened her eyes.

Finn was looking down at her, breathing heavily, his face dripping wet. They were back in Albert's boat.

'You … you saved me,' Becky mumbled.

Finn shook his head. 'I got you out of the water, but Lord Thistlewick saved you.'

'W-what?'

Finn pointed at Becky's hand and she saw the bottle there.

'That bottle was glowing. I've never seen a colour like it before. Whatever *The Grimwood*'s curse was, I think Lord Thistlewick's bottle stopped it from hurting you.'

10

Time Is Ticking

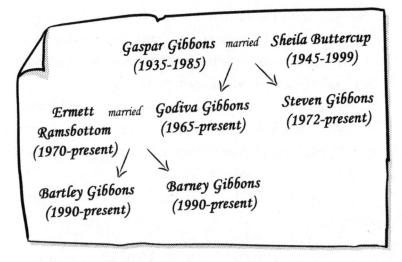

Gaspar Gibbons married *Sheila Buttercup*
(1935-1985)   *(1945-1999)*

Ermett married *Godiva Gibbons*   *Steven Gibbons*
Ramsbottom *(1965-present)*   *(1972-present)*
(1970-present)

Bartley Gibbons *Barney Gibbons*
(1990-present)   *(1990-present)*

An extract from the Thistlewick family tree

Becky uncorked the two bottles and stood them side-by-side on the desk in the harbour hut. She pulled a blanket tightly around herself as Finn rummaged in some boxes.

He pulled out a pack of candles and box of matches and looked at Becky.

'Place the candles in a square around the bottles,' she said.

Finn did so, then struck a match and lit each one. He stood back.

Becky watched the flames flicker gently and crossed her fingers. *Please let this be it.*

'How long do we wait?' asked Finn.

'As long as it takes.'

Less than a minute later the left-hand bottle – the first they had found – started to shake. Becky took a gulp of air and held it. The second bottle was soon vibrating too. Their movements grew bigger as the two bottles heated up, until they were about ready to fall over.

'We don't want them to smash, do we?' asked Finn.

Becky shook her head. She grabbed the neck of one bottle and Finn took the other. They tried to hold them still, but they continued to shake.

Let this be it, Becky thought. *Lord Thistlewick's ghost. Please!*

'Guuuhhh!' yelled the noise from the bottle.

Finn turned wide-eyed to Becky. 'It's worked! Lord This—'

'No. Shhh!' Becky hissed.

A voice rose out of the bottles. It was louder than before, more urgent, more excited, but the same deep voice. '*The very thing that saved me from this death nearly caused another. Find it and you'll find these bottles' brother.*'

Becky slowly closed her eyes and groaned. 'There's another bottle.'

A fumbling sound came from the harbour hut door. She froze.

'It's Granddad,' Finn realised.

'Pass me the bottles, quick!'

Becky took them from Finn, pushed the corks back

in and shoved them under her blanket just as the old fisherman entered.

But he wasn't alone. Waddling in behind him was Godiva Gibbons.

'Hello, you two. Are you OK, Becky, wrapped up like that?'

'Yes, I was just a bit cold.'

'That's why we lit the candles,' Finn added, hurriedly blowing them out.

Becky's eyes met Godiva, whose expression was unreadable.

Albert followed her gaze. 'Oh, this is Mrs Ramsbottom. A tourist. We got chatting in the pub.'

Becky and Finn exchanged a frown. Why was she calling herself Mrs Ramsbottom again?

'We were talking about the lightning in the market this morning. Did you hear about it?' Godiva's voice was sickly sweet.

'Apparently, folk are standing around the place it struck, calling for Lord Thistlewick,' Albert explained. 'It's a sign from him, no doubt, but they don't need to worry themselves. He will appear in his own good time, and probably to the true Thistlewickian.' His bright eyes fell on Becky. 'I was telling Mrs Ramsbottom about you. Said I had the true Thistlewickian in my hut. She wanted to come and say hello.'

'Hello,' Becky said flatly, panic bubbling inside. Only

her blanket stopped Godiva from seeing Lord Thistle-wick's bottles.

'Well, well, the *true* Thistlewickian.' Godiva beamed a huge fake smile. 'But you haven't met *him* yet?'

'No.'

'It will be a shame if he doesn't arrive before the end of the fair tonight, won't it?' said Godiva.

'Yes, it is always quite a spectacle. Lord Thistlewick would love it, I'm sure,' said Albert.

'I hear it could even be quite destructive.' Although her smile was still fixed, Godiva's eyes were like daggers staring into Becky.

'Ay?' Albert frowned.

'I mean, dramatic. Quite dramatic.'

Godiva held out a hand to Becky. Becky kept hers firmly inside the blanket, holding tightly onto the bottles. Godiva moved her hand up to Becky's shoulder and pressed it firmly.

'A pleasure to meet you, Becky.' Godiva pulled her close and hissed, 'Get me my treasure!'

'Ay?' asked Albert again.

'I was just saying how lovely she looks.'

Becky pulled away from Godiva. 'We have to go. Come on, Finn.'

Glaring and still wrapped in the blanket, she stormed out of the harbour hut, straight past the two clowns, standing either side of the door.

As Finn caught up with Becky halfway up the harbour steps, she turned back to the clowns. 'Going to follow us, are you?'

They looked at each other, stared back at Becky, then disappeared inside the hut.

***

Becky and Finn saw the pile of books on the library floor before they saw Jimmy. They walked around it and found their friend sitting amongst them.

'We just met Godiva at the harbour,' said Becky. 'She was lovely and threatening.'

Jimmy looked up and his face cracked into a grin.

'What is it?' asked Finn.

'Remember what Godiva's clowns are called?'

'Bartley and Barney,' said Becky.

Jimmy nodded. 'They're her sons.'

'You're joking!'

'No. I've been reading these.' He gestured at all the books. 'I haven't found any more near-death experiences, but I have found out more about Godiva. I've just been reading the Thistlewick family tree. Look.'

He pointed to a yellowing page with lots of names covering it. Near the top was Lord Thistlewick and under that his daughter Coral-Anne, married to Grinlin Gibbons. At the bottom, Becky saw Godiva's name. She had married a man called Ermett Ramsbottom, and they had two sons: Bartley and Barney.

'That explains why she's bossing them about so much,' said Becky. 'They're weird. Why do they never talk?'

'It definitely makes them more creepy,' said Finn. 'If Godiva married Ermett, is her surname Ramsbottom, like she's been telling people?'

'According to *The Thistlewick Family: An Intimate Biog-raphy*, she wanted to stay a Gibbons, so she made Ermett take *her* last name instead,' said Jimmy.

'I guess she's using Ramsbottom to hide who she really is, then. What else did you find out?' asked Becky.

'Godiva runs a construction company in England, and Ermett owns Ermett's Transportation Limited. His company delivered all the fair equipment to Thistlewick.'

'So … Godiva owns lots of machinery and can transport it easily. She really can destroy Thistlewick if she wants to,' said Finn.

Becky felt the panic inside her rise up again, like a kettle coming to the boil. They really did have to stop Godiva.

Jimmy nodded. 'And she will if we don't find this second bottle.'

Becky took the two bottles out from their hiding place under the blanket.

Jimmy's mouth fell open. 'How did you…? Does that mean…?'

'No. We tried heating them up and got another voice.'

'*The very thing that saved me from this death nearly caused another*,' Finn recounted. 'What does that mean?'

'Well, what saved him from the death you're talking about?' asked Jimmy.

Becky and Finn told him Albert's story about the cursed ship, and how Becky had found the bottle.

'Wow, that sounds dangerous! But well done, Becky!' said Jimmy. 'And don't you see? The thing that saved him from death was the sorceress. She must be connected to another of his near-death experiences.'

'Then the voice said, *Find it and you'll find these bottles' brother*,' Becky explained. 'So if we find this sorceress, we'll find the final bottle.'

'Let's hope it's the final one, anyway,' Finn added. 'We only have until tonight.'

Jimmy stood up and went over to a bookshelf on the other side of the library. He came back with three more books.

'I didn't even think to look at these. They're all about sorcery. Maybe they'll contain information about Lord Thistlewick's sorceress. Let's take one each.'

He handed Becky and Finn books.

Becky unwrapped her blanket, laid it on the floor and sat down on it. She opened *Sorcerers: Good or Bad?* to a random page and flicked through. It contained the biographies of various people who may or may not have had supernatural powers, and may or may not have used them for evil. It would take ages to read about all of them. Becky turned to the back and found an index. She ran a finger down it and came to *Thistlewick, Lord, p. 83*. She quickly flicked back through the book. Page 83 was about a sorceress called Mitexi Shelldrake.

As Becky read through Mitexi's biography, her eyes lit up.

'I've got her! Mitexi Shelldrake. She saved Lord Thistlewick from *The Grimwood*'s curse, but before that she tried to curse him herself.'

'Does it say where we can find her?' asked Finn.

'She'll be long dead by now, won't she?' Jimmy pointed out.

'It says she chose to live in the darkest, most ghostly part of the Forest of Shadows,' Becky read. 'Maybe she's still there as a ghost. I'll ask Willow. Willow?'

'Yes?'

'Aaahhh!' Finn threw his book in the air as Willow floated up and out of it.

'I'm getting better at being spooky, aren't I? How can I help?'

'Do you know if there's a ghost called Mitexi Shelldrake on Thistlewick?' asked Becky.

'I am not sure. I haven't heard that name before.'

'When she was alive, she lived in the forest,' said Jimmy.

'Oh, well, the forest is where many of the evil ghosts live. I haven't been back there since we escaped from Thicket House, so I know very little about them.'

'I know all the rumours about how dangerous the forest is, but can you take me in there?' asked Becky. 'In the ghost world, I mean? I think Mitexi has Lord Thistlewick's final bottle. We need to find it, and quick.'

'I am not sure,' said Willow. 'The last living person who was allowed into the ghost world was Eric Pockle. I will have to ask for permission.'

In the blink of an eye, the ghost girl was gone. While they waited for her to return, Finn and Becky helped Jimmy put the books back. She wasn't sure how to feel and stayed silent.

'Yes.' The soft voice came from behind Becky. She turned to look at Willow. 'We all voted and you are allowed to visit the ghost world. Everyone thinks it's important.'

Now Becky felt excitement mixing with her panic. 'Thank you!'

'Let's go, then,' said Finn.

'I am afraid you cannot come,' said Willow. 'I am only allowed to take Becky with me.'

***

Becky stared up at the tall, twisted trees of the Forest of Shadows.

Willow placed a hand on Becky's shoulder. She felt a warm ball of energy burst through her, like a pleasant electric shock.

'Welcome to the ghost world, Becky.' Willow smiled.

Becky looked around, expecting to see lots more ghosts like Willow, but they were still alone.

She frowned. 'Am I definitely in the ghost world? Everything looks the same and there are no other ghosts.'

'We do not like coming near the forest if we can avoid it,' said Willow. 'But can you see me?'

'Yes.'

'Then you are, because I stopped showing myself when I touched your shoulder. I am now invisible in the living world.'

'Wow!' Willow looked just the same to Becky. She turned back to the trees and saw they were now highlighted by a green glow. It made the forest seem even creepier. 'Does that mean I'm invisible too?'

'No, only ghosts can be invisible. You are still very much a part of the living world, but you can now also see the ghost world.'

Becky nodded. She thought about what the book had said: Mitexi Shelldrake lived in the darkest, most ghostly part of the forest. If she was still there now, it wasn't going to be easy to find her.

Becky tensed her fists and stepped between two trees and into the Forest of Shadows.

11

The Ghost Hand

A woman who proves that sorcerers are not all bad is Mitexi Shelldrake.

Initially, she seemed to be heading down a dark path.

Lord Adlestrop and Lord Thistlewick, two rivalling adventurers, had a bet over which of them could find the most undiscovered islands. Lord Thistlewick was clearly winning the bet, so Lord Adlestrop employed Mitexi Shelldrake to kill him.

However, Lord Thistlewick managed to find the goodness within Mitexi...

From *Sorcerers: Good or Bad?* by Ecived Evitarran

Becky scanned her EMF detector left and right. Even though they weren't far into the forest, it still gave high readings: 0.5 to the right and 0.7 to the left. Maybe Willow was affecting it.

'Which way?' asked the ghost girl.

'We have get to the most ghostly part, so whichever way has the highest number, I guess.'

Becky ducked under a twisted branch and moved off left. Willow floated effortlessly through the darkness beside her, her silvery glow lighting the way.

After a while, Becky held up the EMF detector again. Left still gave a reading of 0.7, but now right was 0.8. They changed direction, and Becky weaved around the thick trees, trying to avoid tripping over dead roots.

She heard a crunching and rustling behind her.

'Hold on,' she whispered.

They stopped and listened. Becky saw a flash of green – but not the green glow of the forest, this was brighter.

'It's Bartley.' She puffed out her cheeks. 'I'm fed up of being followed by Godiva's clowns.'

'Stay there,' said Willow. 'I will get rid of him.'

The ghost girl soared back through the trees.

Becky pressed herself against a tree, out of sight. A minute later Willow returned, grinning.

'It worked! I can be a scary ghost!'

'What did you do?' asked Becky.

'I kept myself invisible and whispered his name in his ear. That made him jump. I told him his mum was angry with him. Then I flashed my image on for just a second and pulled my scariest face. He ran screaming out of the forest!'

'I didn't hear a scream,' said Becky.

Willow smiled. 'He's a clown. He did it silently.'

They moved off again and Becky took another scan. Now towards the right gave a reading of 1.1.

'That's high,' said Becky. 'There must be ghosts nearby.'

'There are. Look!'

At first Becky couldn't see what Willow meant. Her heart jumped when she made out several black shadows with faint green glows around them.

'Are they spectres?'

'No,' said Willow. 'Look at their shapes.'

Becky stared and recognised the shapes of humans. There were lots of them, hovering behind the trees all around her. She couldn't see any eyes, but was sure they were all looking at her, which made her shiver. In any other situation, Becky knew it would be sensible to get away from these strange beings, but she had to move towards them, to get to the most ghostly part of the forest.

'Let's keep going.'

They walked on past several ugly trees. Not only did the shadows follow, but new ones seemed to join.

A buzzing noise started in Becky's ears. She shook her head, thinking it was coming from inside. Then she realised – it was voices, whispering and hissing from all around her.

She stopped and listened.

'*The girl, get the girl!*'

'*We could use her.*'

'*Trap! Kill!*'

'*No, alive. We can use her better alive.*'

'*We want her dead!*'

'*No, alive.*'

'*Dead!*'

'*Yes, dead!*'

Becky turned to Willow and tried to speak, but no words came out. These things – these evil ghosts – wanted to kill her, and they were surrounding her, hundreds of them!

'It's OK,' said Willow, floating close. 'They would only attack if they all actually agreed whether to kill you or not. They never all agree.'

'Great…' Becky mouthed.

She quickened her pace, the green glow now bright enough to light up the whole forest, strangely making it easier to see.

Becky held out the EMF detector all the time, waving it around and darting in whichever direction gave the highest reading. It kept getting higher: 1.2, 1.7, 2.3 …

The voices got louder and more and more shadow-ghosts joined in. '*Dead! Alive! Dead! Dead! Alive! Dead! Dead!*'

Becky swerved to avoid hitting her head on a low-lying branch and walked straight through a black shadow.

'*DEAD!*' Its voice ran through her like an ice chill.

3.5, the EMF detector now read. She kept going in as straight a line as the trees would allow. 5.1.

'How high can the numbers go?' asked Willow.

'I don't know.'

As if the EMF detector was answering the question itself, its screen changed to: ERROR.

'Alive! Dead! Alive! Alive! Dead!'

Becky looked up. Ahead was a beam of sunlight, and she strode towards it, desperate to get away from the shadows and take in natural light again.

She reached a clearing into which the sun shone. She closed her eyes and let the sun's rays hit her. Then everything went dark.

'Dead! Dead! Dead!'

Becky opened her eyes, but she couldn't see a thing. She swung her head around, but Willow was nowhere – just darkness.

'Dead! Dead! Dead! Dead!' The voices were all she could hear, filling her ears and her mind.

'Willow?!' she yelled, realising she couldn't hear any of them saying 'alive' now.

'Dead! Dead! DEAD!'

Becky's heart pounded. She tried to breathe, but every breath was sucked back out of her by the swirling blackness. Her arms were yanked away from her, like the ghosts were trying to pull them off.

'DEAD! DEAD! DEAAAAAAD!'

Becky tried to kick out, but now the ghosts grabbed her legs too and she was tossed in the air, being pulled in four different directions. The blackness and the voices consumed her.

'AWAY, FOUL CREATURES! AWAY!'

Whose voice was this?

'GET AWAY OR FACE MY WRATH!'

Becky fell to the ground, her arms and legs released. She blinked and saw a few cracks of light appearing in the black.

'AWAY!' the voice commanded again.

As quickly as they had surrounded her, the shadow-ghosts disappeared. Shaking, Becky stood.

Willow shot up to her. 'Becky! Are you OK? I'm sorry, I couldn't stop them.'

Becky looked around.

'Whose voice was that? Who stopped them attacking me?'

Willow pointed to a small building standing on the other side of the clearing. Becky wasn't sure how it *was* still standing – the outside walls were the colour of mould and so cracked it looked like a powerful sneeze might knock them over.

The door was open and someone wrapped in a thick black shawl stood – no, floated – there. Only her face was visible, a large nose extending out from it. While her shawl was surrounded by a silver glow, her nose was highlighted in a sickly green.

'Come in, quickly!'

Becky looked at Willow, who nodded. She stepped in through the doorway, Willow by her side.

Without anyone touching the door, it slammed shut.

Becky felt very uneasy. The room was cold and lined with glass jars containing slimy grey objects. She tried not to look too closely at them. In the centre of the room was a round table, with what looked like a cauldron standing on it.

'The forest is in a state of unrest,' said the woman, her voice low and dark. 'The evil ghosts here are planning something.'

She sat down behind the cauldron and peered at Becky, although Becky couldn't quite see her eyes.

'Thank you for saving me,' said Becky quietly. 'Are … are you Mitexi Shelldrake?'

'I am. And what brings a living human and a silver ghost to my house?'

'Becky is looking for Lord Thistlewick,' said Willow.

Mitexi turned to her suspiciously.

'For his bottles,' Becky added.

Suddenly Mitexi leant forwards and Becky saw her bright green eyes now. 'Then you are here because you have found two already.'

'Yes. How did you know?'

Mitexi signalled for Becky to sit on the chair opposite her, and it creaked under her weight. Still unsure how to feel, she pulled the two bottles out of her pocket and placed them on the table.

Mitexi nodded at them. 'Before I became a ghost

myself, I helped Lord Thistlewick to split his ghost between these bottles.'

'How did he do it?' asked Becky.

'It is something I would not wish on my worst enemy,' said Mitexi. 'Too painful, and involving the most excruciating magic that I won't dare talk about. But Lord Thistlewick knew it was important. Please, do tell me what you did to get the bottles.'

Becky explained how she had found out about the prophecy, about the message on the fallen rock, about Godiva, and about the challenge of finding the bottles. Mitexi stared at her closely and nodded and kept saying, 'Good, good.'

'Did you know where the bottles were?' asked Becky.

'Yes. I hid them myself, following Lord Thistlewick's instructions exactly. He wanted the person who found them to go through some of the challenges he did when he was alive. My last job was to create that prophecy about the rock.'

'You were the fortune teller, all those years ago?'

Mitexi nodded.

'So did you make the rock fall off as well?'

'No, Becky, you did that.'

'I couldn't have. I hardly touched it. Godiva tried really hard and it didn't budge for her.'

'A touch was all it needed, but from the right person,' Mitexi explained. When Becky frowned, she continued,

'The rock was not held by normal forces. I placed a spell on it, so that it would only fall if the right person touched it: someone who wasn't thinking only of taking Lord Thistlewick's treasure, but wanted to protect it from evil. It seems that person is you.'

Mitexi reached her spidery hand into the cauldron. Out of it, she pulled out a bottle. She placed it on the table. Becky gasped at the round shape and thin neck with the golden letter T carved into it.

'The third bottle!'

Something flickered inside it and the bottle seemed to glow.

'The first two bottles link to Lord Thistlewick's near-death experiences,' said Becky. 'Does this one?'

'It does.' Mitexi leaned closer still and Becky saw that the pupils in her eyes were diamond shaped, almost snake-like. 'Because when we first met, I tried to kill him.'

How Lord Thistlewick nearly died

(according to Mitexi Shelldrake)

I was in desperate need of money when Lord Adlestrop employed me to kill Lord Thistlewick.

Lord Thistlewick set off in search of Leech Island, which no human had visited before, so I followed him. I hypnotised the sharks in the sea below his boat to attack him.

But he was too skilful. He knew exactly how to battle against the creatures.

When Lord Thistlewick arrived at the island, he sat on a beach and lit a fire. I cursed that fire, turning it into fire-snakes.

He fought the creatures off using only his own spit.

After failing twice, I watched Lord Thistlewick move into a cave to camp for the night. Inside it, lucky for me, he encountered a huge, angry spectre.

I stood back and watched the spectre shoot at him, trying to take all his energy. I thought the spectre would do my job for me, but Lord Thistlewick defeated it in minutes.

The next morning, Lord Thistlewick entered the forest at the centre of Leech Island. As I followed, I realised why the island had got its name. The ground was covered in them. But forests are where I am most at home, so I found I was able to avoid being sucked.

Lord Thistlewick did not fare so well. He ended up surrounded by monstrous blood-sucking leeches. His only way to avoid them was to climb a tree.

This was my chance. When he was halfway up, I put a spell on the tree, making its branches reach out and grab him. The branches curled around him and held his whole body tight. One wrapped around his neck, slowly strangling him.

I climbed up next to him. His eyes were bulging in pain and he couldn't speak, but he stared straight at me. One by one, I enchanted the leeches to fly up the tree and attach themselves to his body. They could suck his blood out. It would be a slow and painful death.

However, he managed to whisper through gritted

teeth, 'You do not have to do this. There are kinder ways to use your skills.'

I was taken aback. I lowered my hand and replied, 'I am being paid. I need the money.'

'You can make a better living,' he said. 'Join me. I am creating a new island, a happy island. There will be a place for you there. You can help me do good.'

We talked, all the while the leeches sucking his blood away, and he persuaded me to give up Lord Adlestrop's evil plans.

I freed him from the leeches and we escaped Leech Island together. I moved to Thistlewick Island soon after, and supported him in every way I could. Lord Thistlewick was a remarkable man. He taught me how to be kind.

'Wow!' said Becky.

'Lord Thistlewick valued kindness and goodness above all else. I can see those qualities in you, Becky. So, I am giving you this bottle. Take it.'

Becky reached out and gently placed her hand around the bottle's neck. But it went straight through, and a chill ran up her hand.

Mitexi gave a toothy smile. 'When I died, I took the bottle with me into the ghost world. Only the person who is truly meant to have it can take it back into the living world.'

Becky looked at Willow, who shook her head.

'How do I do that?'

'You need to separate your inner body from your outer body,' said Mitexi.

Becky flinched. 'You're not going to cut me open, are you?'

'No, no! Place your hand firmly on the table.'

Becky put her left hand down. She couldn't stop it trembling.

'Now focus your whole mind on that hand. Tell it to pick up the bottle, but keep it firmly pressed against the table.'

Becky frowned, but did as Mitexi said. *Lift off the table!* she thought. *Pick up the bottle!*

She stared at her hand. It lifted up and—

'No!' said Mitexi. 'It cannot move off the table.'

'But how—?'

'Hold your left hand down with your right hand. Tell the right to keep it held down, but tell the left to lift.'

Becky puffed out her cheeks. *Right hand, put all your weight on the left hand. Left hand, lift, lift, lift!*

She blinked. For a second she saw double – like her left hand had ten fingers instead of five. She shook her head and it returned to normal.

'Did you see that?' asked Willow.

Becky looked uncertainly at Mitexi.

'That was it!' the ghost shouted. 'I knew you were the one. Keep going, Becky.'

Right hand – push all your weight down. Left hand, lift. Lift! LIFT!

This time, a pale, see-through version of Becky's left hand lifted away from the one still pressed against the table.

'Is … is that like a ghost hand?'

'You can think of it like that,' said Mitexi. 'Keep going.'

Lift! LIFT!

The hand rose into the air, and a see-through arm went with it. Becky didn't dare blink. This was amazing!

Move towards the bottle.

The hand did so.

Pick it up!

It was the weirdest sensation. Becky felt the wood

of the table against her solid left hand, but as the see-through hand grasped the bottle, she also felt its coldness – two different sensations coming from the same hand.

'Now bring the bottle towards you,' Mitexi urged.

Bring me the bottle!

The ghost hand pulled the bottle to her, until it was placed between the fingers of her solid living hand. As her see-through hand merged back into the one on the table, she felt solid glass. Moving her right hand off, she let her left hand pick up the bottle. It felt surprisingly heavy.

Becky blinked. 'It's … it's real!'

Mitexi sat back in her chair. 'You have brought the bottle back into the living world!'

'Well done, Becky!' said Willow. 'Well done!'

Becky breathed deeply and placed the third bottle next to the others. 'And this is the final bottle?'

'All the anicent books show that a ghost can only be split into three parts,' said Mitexi. 'Now you must take them all to the beach under Watcher's Cliff. It is Lord Thistlewick's favourite part of the island, so he will be pleased to see it when you bring his ghost back together.'

12

The Fire and the Tunnel

FUN FACT

Lord Thistlewick's favourite number was four.

He liked to collect four of everything: four purple cloaks, four grand boats, four pet kittens...

From *The Thistlewick Family: An Intimate Biography* (300th Anniversary Edition) by Sandi Foot

Becky, Jimmy and Finn stood at the bottom of Watcher's Cliff and waited for Willow. The ghost girl soared back over from *The Caspian*, still anchored just offshore.

'Godiva and her sons are on board. They are looking at maps of Thistlewick.'

'Then we need to be quick and quiet,' said Becky. 'Once Lord Thistlewick appears, though, we won't need to worry about them.'

Finn placed some old bits of wood on the sand.

'Even more, Finn.' Becky knelt down to help him. 'We'll need a lot of energy to bring the three bottles together.'

They put down all the wood they had brought, then

Finn took out a bottle of oil and poured it over the pile.

'Stand back,' he said.

Becky stepped away. She struck a match and threw it onto the wood. Flames immediately burst out from it, their warmth filling the air.

Jimmy took the three uncorked bottles and carefully placed them right in front of the fire.

They all waited. Becky stared at the bright orange flames reflected in the bottles. She was getting used to the feeling of nervous excitement, but now she knew they had all the bottles – that any second she really would meet Lord Thistlewick – her heart thumped extra hard.

The bottles started to shake and Becky held her breath. She looked to the others, whose eyes were wide and fixed on the bottles.

As they shook more violently, a spark from the fire shot at Becky and she jumped back to avoid it.

'Careful, Becky!' said Willow.

A whole flame fired out at her now. She stumbled and fell to the ground as the flame rose up in the air. It curled around and changed shape, forming a white-hot snake.

Becky tensed, ready for it to attack. She crawled back next to Jimmy, but the snake followed. She felt fear burning through her as it moved its newly-formed head up next to her. A red tongue flickered out of the mouth.

'*Mitexi thought three was the most,*' the snake said in the deep, familiar voice of Lord Thistlewick, crackling and spitting. *'But I wanted more for my ghost. I split myself into four. Your greatest challenge lies through this door.'*

'Door? What door?' asked Finn.

The fire-snake looked at him. It tilted its head left and slithered along the ground away from the rest of the fire.

'Quick, follow it!' cried Becky.

They charged after the fire-snake. It led them to the far side of the beach, to a large pile of rocks stacked up against the cliff. The snake turned its head back to Becky, hissed, then shot through the rocks. With a spark of white and a puff of smoke it was gone.

'Is there a door behind those rocks?' asked Jimmy.

'Let's shift them and find out!' said Becky.

They set about clearing the rocks, chucking the smaller ones away and lifting the heavier ones between them. It was taking a long time and Becky worried that Godiva could discover what they were up to at any moment, so Willow kept an eye on *The Caspian*.

They must have lifted a hundred rocks by the time they started to see the part of the cliff the rocks had been covering. Becky panted heavily, but kept going.

'Look!' said Finn, as they moved away an extra-heavy rock between the three of them.

'It's a hole in the cliff!' Jimmy realised.

They dropped the rock and Becky ran up to the hole. It was pitch-black inside, but big enough for a person to fit in. 'Like a cave entrance. A door?'

Willow joined them. She peered in through the hole. Her body started to flicker, then she disappeared all together.

'Willow?' asked Becky.

The ghost girl reappeared next to her, still flickering. 'I lost my energy then. I cannot go in there. Something is stopping me – something dark.'

Becky looked at Jimmy and Finn, who both stood motionless. Becky clenched her fists and walked towards the hole. She fumbled in her pocket, pulled out a torch and shone it into the darkness.

'It's a tunnel,' she said.

She ran back to the fire, pulled off her jumper and wrapped the still-hot bottles inside it. She handed the jumper to Finn.

'Keep hold of this. Make sure Godiva doesn't get it.'

He nodded and put it in his rucksack.

Becky stepped inside the tunnel entrance and felt the slippery rock under her feet.

'Are you sure about this?' asked Jimmy behind her.

'No. But we've come this far. I have to find the fourth bottle.'

'You're not doing it without me.' Finn stepped into the tunnel.

'Or me…' Jimmy joined them, although Becky saw his whole body was tense.

'I am sorry I cannot come in,' said Willow.

'That's OK,' said Becky. 'Can you stay guard and make sure Godiva doesn't—'

'You three! Where are you going?' Godiva!

Willow disappeared as Becky saw Godiva wading through the water towards the beach. Their noise had obviously caught her attention.

'Quick, block up the hole behind us!' said Becky.

They began piling up rocks in front of the hole, blocking themselves in – and Godiva out. But the pile barely reached their knees by the time the woman got to the hole.

'Lord Thistlewick's treasure is in there … isn't it?' Godiva hissed, out of breath. 'All this time and it was under my nose!'

Becky just stood and glared at her.

'You're not even going to touch that treasure. It's all mine!' Godiva started to step over the pile of rocks, but Finn blocked her.

'Really?' She gave a shrill laugh. 'O, Bartley, Barney!'

The clowns splashed through the water towards the beach. Becky looked to Jimmy and Finn. They couldn't win against the clowns. Maybe they should run down the tunnel and hope they could lose Godiva and her sons.

The clowns were halfway up the beach when Jimmy gasped. Becky saw it too – the fallen rock from Watcher's Cliff, sitting in the middle of the beach, started to move towards the clowns. It rolled through the middle of them, knocking them over like ten-pins. Becky couldn't help laughing. Whatever spell Mitexi had put on the rock, it was helping them. The rock picked up speed. It was coming straight for the tunnel entrance.

'Aaahhh!' Godiva yelled, diving out of the way.

BANG! The rock slammed in place, blocking up the hole.

The only light now came from Becky's torch.

'You will bring me that treasure!' she heard Godiva yelling from the other side of the rock. 'Every last bit of it! And before the fireworks display tonight! Or I will destroy your island, every last bit of *it*!'

***

They walked down the tunnel, following the dim beam from Becky's torch. The rock walls around them were slimy with seaweed and water dripped from the ceiling. None of them said a word – they were too tense to talk.

A minute later they came to a split in the tunnel. There were now two paths to choose between.

'Which one?' asked Jimmy.

'Let's split up. I'll take this one, you two take that one,' Finn suggested.

'No, we need to stick together,' Becky said firmly. 'Anything could be around the corner.'

She pulled out her EMF detector and scanned down

the right-hand path. 0.5 flashed up on her screen. She moved over to the left-hand path and did the same. 0.9.

'This way seems more ghostly. Come on.'

The path took them into another, much narrower tunnel. Becky's feet skidded on the ground and she felt herself lift into the air. She tried to grab onto the walls but they were too slimy.

'Ahhh!'

A firm hand grabbed her shoulder. It was Finn, and he stopped her fall. After that she trod carefully, shining the torch around to find the safest path, and making sure she did the same for Jimmy and Finn following her.

When they came to a bend Becky held her hand out and the other two stopped. She crept slowly round it, certain there would be something nasty hiding there.

Ahead was a faint glow.

'Is it the end of the tunnel?' whispered Finn.

They moved towards the glow. Becky realised it came from a long stretch of greenish-grey water, running through a cavern. She reached the edge of the water and it lapped gently against her feet.

Finn bent down and dipped his hand in. 'It's warm.'

'Careful! There could be something in there,' said Becky.

'There is,' said Jimmy. 'A boat.'

Jimmy was pointing to a small rowing boat floating to their left.

'Let's see where it takes us.' said Becky.

She climbed in, followed by Finn and Jimmy.

'You sit at the front and guide us this time,' Finn told Jimmy as he took one oar and Becky the other.

'This boat feels just as old as *Patch* – older, maybe,' said Finn.

'Let's hope it holds together better than *Patch*,' said Becky.

Jimmy looked at her with nervous eyes.

They started rowing through the water and made easy progress, with no rocks to steer around this time.

'What's that in the water?' Jimmy pointed.

Becky gasped at the a triangular shape floating ahead. 'It's … it's a shark fin.'

'It's moving around like in a film,' said Finn. 'Looks fake to me.'

'I … I'm not sure.' Becky had a nagging feeling about what was really happening, but she hoped she was wrong.

A second fin appeared, then a third, circling around the boat.

Jimmy shot backwards then, nearly landing on Finn's lap.

'Watch it!'

'It-it … it's…' Jimmy stuttered.

Becky saw the very real head of a shark, its razor teeth bared as it rose out of the water.

13

Sharks

Many people think that only humans can become ghosts. But, of course, the ghost world is full of other creatures: ghost elephants, ghost dolphins, ghost hamsters, ghost slugs.

One of the best ghostly encounters I ever had was with a cow called Jeff.

From *My Life With Ghosts* by Eric Pockle,
published after the author's death

The water under the boat rocked as the shark leapt through the water, revealing a shiny body twice the size of Becky. It splashed back into the water, sending a wave crashing into the boat and soaking them instantly.

'Whoa!' cried Finn. 'That's definitely not fake.'

Jimmy had now managed to squeeze himself behind Becky and Finn.

'It's OK, Jimmy. I know what this is,' Becky said calmly. 'This is the challenge Lord Thistlewick faced when Mitexi hypnotised sharks to attack him.'

'They're going to attack us?!'

'No. See that green glow? They're ghost sharks, so they can't actually attack.'

Crunch!

Becky felt a tugging on her oar, and when she lifted it up she gasped – the paddle at the end had been ripped off, leaving her with just a stick of wood. She slowly leant over the side of the boat. Smiling up at her was the wide, angry face of a shark, chomping the paddle into splinters between its ghost teeth.

More bullet-like faces appeared around the boat, all smiling up, ready to bite.

Becky looked at Finn. 'Row, Finn, row!'

He plunged his oar back in the water and pushed the boat forwards.

'Shark straight ahead!' Jimmy called.

Its jaws were open wide, about to chomp up the front of the boat. Finn switched sides, narrowly avoiding the mouth of another shark as he shoved the oar back in the water.

The boat swerved right, passing by the snapping jaws of the shark in front of them.

Becky saw a large shimmering box hanging above the water ahead of them. 'What's that?'

'A cage!' Finn's eyes lit up. 'It'll keep us safe from the sharks.'

He kept rowing, moving his oar left and right and left to avoid the sharks.

The boat jolted as something hit it from underneath. 'Aaahhhhh!' Becky cried.

Glowing white teeth the size of fingers appeared between her feet, chomping into the wood at the bottom of the boat. She thrust her stick of oar down but it just passed through the shark's ghostly nose.

Water flooded into the boat through the hole it had created. Becky felt it seeping through her socks. She put a foot over the hole, but couldn't stop the water rising quickly upwards. They were still several metres away from the cage.

'Not again!' yelled Finn, still furiously trying to row.

'Jimmy, help me get rid of this water!' said Becky.

Jimmy joined her in scooping the water out, but more water flooded in than they could remove.

'Quick, Finn, quick!'

The back end of the boat sank down and a shark leapt up and nearly caught Jimmy.

'AAAHHHHH!'

He shot to the front of the boat, and his weight lifted the back end up again.

They were close enough to the cage now to touch it. Becky jumped up to join Jimmy at the front, stretching out and grabbing hold of the cage door. It clicked open.

Becky looked down. The waves the sharks were making tossed the boat around, but she thought she could make it into the cage. She gritted her teeth and leapt out of the boat.

Her feet landed on the solid metal floor of the cage.

She let out a long breath. The sudden movement excited the sharks, though – they started fighting each other to squeeze into the gap between the boat and the cage.

'Come on, Jimmy!'

He looked at the sharks and shook his head.

'Grab my hand. I'll pull you across.'

She stretched out and he gripped her arm.

'Ready? One, two, three.' Becky yanked him out of the boat.

As he flew through the air a shark leapt up, its nose brushing against his leg. Jimmy collapsed into the cage.

'Now you, Finn!'

Finn put down the oar and stood up.

A shark – the biggest of the lot – burst out of the water and dived towards him.

'Finn, look out!'

The huge shark caught the back of the boat in its teeth. It tossed the boat up into the air. Finn started to roll out of it and Becky screamed – he'd be shark food in seconds!

'Jump!' Becky yelled.

He threw himself out of the boat, his arms flailing about, trying to grab hold of the cage. Becky managed to grasp his left hand and pulled with all her might.

Finn's top half was pressed to the floor of the cage, but his legs dangled out over the side. A shark smiled up at him, opened its jaws and clamped onto his foot.

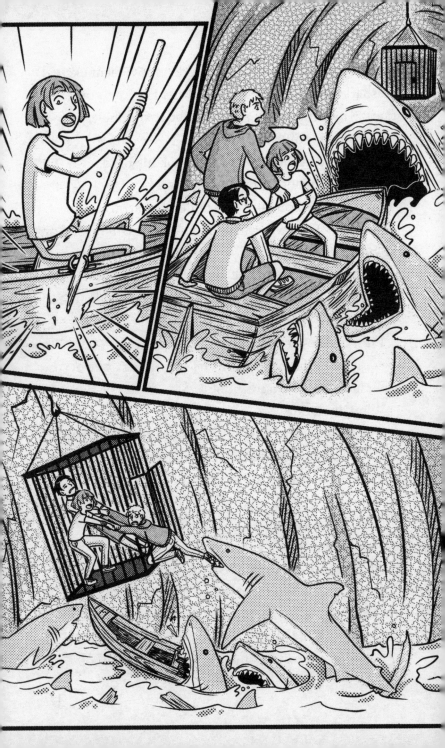

'Get off! Get off!' cried Finn, eyes screwed up tight.

'NOOO!' Becky yelled.

Jimmy took Finn's other arm and they both yanked him towards them. For a second it was like they were playing tug-of-war with the shark, but suddenly Finn came loose. He flew into the cage and landed on top of Becky and Jimmy with a yelp.

Becky rolled out from under him and saw his shoe in the shark's mouth.

'You've definitely still got both feet, right?' she asked.

He wiggled his toes and nodded. The shark's teeth had come close, though – his sock had been shredded.

Becky reached out and pulled the cage door shut. *Clink.*

'AAAHHHHH!' All three of them screamed as the cage jolted downwards.

Becky felt like she had been punched by the weight of the water as the cage plunged into it. She found her friends' hands and held them tight.

A few seconds later the cage fell into dry darkness. *Thud!* It landed on hard ground, throwing them all against the hard metal bars.

The cage door swung open.

Becky slowly stepped out, her arms aching from the rowing and the fall. She held out her hands and felt around.

'Another tunnel, I think.'

'I want this to stop,' said Jimmy in a small voice.

'We can't go back up in the cage, Jimmy. Our only way out is to keep going,' said Becky, trying to ignore the nerves building in her stomach.

She felt in her pocket and found the torch. Water dripped from it, but she tried turning it on and it still worked. They moved along the tunnel.

'What else did Mitexi do to Lord Thistlewick?' asked Finn. 'What are we going to face next?'

Becky thought out loud. 'After the sharks it was fire-snakes, but we've already had that. The next thing was a spectre, but that wasn't part of Mitexi's plan. It just happened to be there.'

'We'd better keep an eye out for big patches of black, just in case,' said Finn.

'Are you sure there's not another way out?'

Becky shone the torch around. 'No, only this tunnel.'

They turned a corner and the sight made Becky stop and stare.

'Wow!' said Finn.

Hanging from the ceiling were hundreds of icicles, some the size of daggers, others like small upside-down trees.

'Stalactites.' Jimmy's wide eyes glowed from their brightness.

Becky turned off her torch. 'There's no way there could be a spectre here with all this ice.'

Finn pointed. 'There's a door on the other side.'

They started to weave around the stalactites. Becky felt their chill as they brushed against her back.

The door was made of thick, dark oak. Stretched across its centre was a long, silver sword. Finn was the first to reach it.

'It's hooked across the door, keeping it locked.'

He took the sword handle and tugged it. With a scraping of metal it came loose.

Clang! It fell from Finn's hand.

'It's really heavy!'

He grasped it again with both hands and picked it up.

'Look at the handle,' said Jimmy, examining it closely.

Carved into it was a golden letter T. Becky nodded confidently. 'It's Lord Thistlewick's sword! We must be getting close to the final bottle.'

Finn looked the object up and down. 'Cool!'

'If it was locking the door, maybe the bottle's behind there.' Becky took hold of the door handle and tugged.

At first it didn't move, but she pulled harder and harder until the door slowly creaked open. They stepped through.

They were now in a wide, empty room, walled in thick, uneven rock with a beam of light coming through a crack in the cliff far above.

'It's a dead end,' said Finn.

'No, look, there's another door over there,' said Jimmy.

He set off towards it.

Becky was about to follow when Finn asked, 'Why's Jimmy got two shadows?'

Becky frowned. It was true: one shadow stretched across the floor to Jimmy's left, the other to his right. She looked at Finn, then at herself – they each only had one shadow.

An awful feeling bubbled in her stomach. 'Jimmy, stand still a minute.'

He stopped and turned to face her, his head tilted uncertainly. But one of his shadows kept moving. It rose off the ground and towered over Jimmy.

'Spectre!' Becky cried.

14

Spectre

It is a mystery why spectres exist. Unlike other ghosts, they do not come from living people or other creatures. Spectres are black masses of pure darkness without a soul. They feed on heat energy, so often hide in people's homes, sucking the heat from their fires and their bodies.

While they are nasty, spectres are generally very small, often the size of a pea, and so not that dangerous. Only a tiny number of spectres will grow bigger than this. If they do, though, they can become deadly, with the power to suck every last drop of energy out of a person.

Because spectres feed on heat energy, they fear anything that could take this away from them.

From *My Life With Ghosts* by Eric Pockle, published after the author's death

'Help!' cried Jimmy. 'Help!'

Becky couldn't see him for the mass of inky blackness swirling around the centre of the room.

'Stay really still, Jimmy!' she called. 'Don't let it take your energy.'

'I-I'm trying, but … but I'm feeling d-dizzy.' Jimmy's voice sounded weak already.

'What do we do?' asked Finn, raising Lord Thistlewick's sword up as if preparing to strike.

'The sword won't work. We need something cold to scare the spectre away,' said Becky, racking her brain for ideas.

'A stalactite!'

'Great idea, Finn!'

The spectre soared up into the air, its many tentacle-like arms stretching out from it. Jimmy cowered below, deathly white, his shaking hands covering his eyes.

One of the spectre's largest tentacles lashed at him.

'Aaahhhhh!'

Jimmy tried to run but stumbled. The inky tentacle grabbed him by the neck and pulled him into the heart of the spectre's blackness.

Now the spectre's own scream mixed with Jimmy's, creating an almost unbearable sound. Becky watched in horror as Jimmy twitched and kicked.

Finn ran to the door they had come through. 'He doesn't have long! I'll get a stalactite. You have to get the spectre away from Jimmy!'

Becky nodded. Trying to turn her fear to anger, she yelled, 'Spectre! *Spectre!*'

Jimmy's body had given up fighting. He spun limply inside the spectre as all his energy was sucked out. Becky remembered when the spectre at Thicket House had captured Finn: once it got you like this, there was no way you could stop it taking your energy.

Becky ran towards it and felt its power forcing her back like a strong wind.

'Spectre!' She pulled out her torch. 'You want energy? Here! This will give you much more!'

She shone the torch directly at it. At first the spectre didn't seem to notice. It was spinning Jimmy round like a tornado and blue sparks shot through its blackness as it screamed.

'SPECTRE!' Becky yelled.

It stopped screaming but kept Jimmy spinning, trying to reach for the torchlight with a free tentacle. Becky shone the light away from the spectre. Another tentacle reached out to grab it. Hands shaking, Becky moved the light again. It was like teasing a dog – a horrific, deadly dog.

'Get the spectre to come through the door!' called Finn.

Becky started to run, waving the torchlight all over the room. This seemed to work – the spectre reached out all its tentacles to catch the light and lost focus on Jimmy, who dropped to the ground, motionless. Becky just hoped he was OK.

She was nearly at the door when the spectre realised where the light was coming from. Instead of chasing the beam of light, it went for the torch itself. Every tentacle shot towards it.

Becky stumbled and swayed as the spectre got near, her energy quickly disappearing. She fell through the doorway and landed on hard rocky ground. The spectre ripped the torch out of her hand and took its power in an instant.

Now almost double its original size, the spectre's tentacles wrapped around Becky's leg and tried to drag her back through the doorway.

She pulled against the spectre, but it was quickly sucking out her energy. It started screaming again. Becky felt so dizzy, like she hadn't eaten in days. The spectre's scream got louder, an awful, piercing sound.

Becky desperately looked around for Finn – where was he? Then she saw him, clinging to the wall on her left, holding Lord Thistlewick's sword up.

'Keep pulling the spectre, Becky!' he yelled through the spectre's noise.

'AAARRRGGGHHH!' With one last tug, she got the spectre through the doorway.

Finn swung the sword. Becky shook her head – attacking the spectre like that wouldn't work.

But, as her vision blurred, she heard several loud cracks above her. The world went black. Then…

Silence.

The spectre had stopped screaming. Becky no longer felt it tugging on her leg. Trembling, she sat up and rubbed her eyes. They came back into focus and she saw Finn holding out a hand. She took it and he pulled her back up.

'W-where's the spectre?'

Finn pointed to the ground. Becky saw a pile of stalactites.

'Did you do that? Cut them down?'

Finn nodded. 'The spectre's trapped under all that ice. It's like a spectre prison.'

'Thank you!' Then Becky remembered. 'Jimmy!'

She staggered back through the door.

15

The Ghost of Becky Evans

Legend has it that a ghost can be made
by a person while they are still alive. The
'ghost' is not separate from the person;
rather, it becomes almost their second
body, fully controlled by the living person.

This is only legend, though. To my
knowledge, no one has ever performed
such an incredible phenomenon.

From *My Life With Ghosts* by Eric Pockle,
published after the author's death

Jimmy was sitting there, trembling but alive. Becky breathed a huge sigh and wrapped her arms around him.

'Let's get out of here,' said Finn.

They helped Jimmy up and made for the second door on the other side of the room. It opened with ease. They found themselves in another tall cavern.

'Whoa!' Becky gasped. Taking up most of the space was a huge tree. There were no leaves, but the many branches coming out from it were like giant spiders.

Jimmy swayed slightly in the doorway, still weak from the spectre's attack.

Becky checked her shadow and those of Jimmy and Finn – they each only had one. 'Don't worry, Jimmy, we'll keep an eye out for spectres.'

He nodded, went over to one side of the cavern and leant against the rocky wall.

'What do we have to do in here?' asked Finn.

Becky craned her neck and looked up to the top of the tree. Light was shining through it. At first she thought it was a beam of light from the outside world, like in the last room. As her eyes focused, though, she saw it was coming from high up in the tree itself: a pale glow, surrounding a small round object.

'It's the fourth bottle!' she realised.

'So we have to climb the tree to get it,' said Finn.

He walked over to the bottom of the tree trunk and went to put his arms around it, but they passed straight through it and met each other in a hug. He frowned.

'It's a ghost tree!' Becky stared up at the bottle at the top of it and mouthed, 'Of course.'

The glow around the bottle must mean it was also in the ghost world, just like the one Mitexi had given her.

'I have to bring it back into the living world.'

'Aaahhh!'

Her heart jumped at Jimmy's cry. She spun around, expecting to see him caught up in another spectre. But there was no second shadow – he was running towards them, away from the wall.

He pointed down at the ground. 'There're leeches …
everywhere … leeches!'

Becky saw a dozen small, brown creatures, each with
its own green glow, right where Jimmy had been sitting.

'Ghost leeches.'

'I thought they were slugs,' said Jimmy. 'Then one
tried to clamp onto my shoe.'

Becky looked around the cavern and realised many
more tiny green glows were coming out of the walls.

'This is the final thing that happened to Lord
Thistlewick on Leech Island,' said Becky. 'I think I have
to get the bottle before the leeches attack us.'

'But how?' asked Finn. 'You can't climb a ghost tree.'

'Not like this I can't.'

Becky planted her feet firmly on the ground. She
focused on the faint glimmer of the bottle far above.
Was this possible? It had to be – there was no other way.

Lift, body, lift! Let me get the bottle! Lift!

Nothing. She held her arms up and tensed her fists.

Lift! I need that bottle! Lift!

Her body shook with effort and she rose up onto
tiptoes. It was no good.

'What are you doing, Becky?' asked Finn.

She looked away from the bottle for a moment,
turning to her friends, who were both frowning at her.

'You're going to have to hold me down.'

Finn raised an eyebrow. 'Why?'

'Just do it.'

He looked to Jimmy, who nodded. They each put a firm hand on Becky's shoulders and placed their own feet on hers.

She stared back at the bottle. *Lift, body! Lift! LIFT!*

Still nothing. Becky sighed. This was impossible.

From around them, she heard the squelching of the leeches getting louder.

'You've got two ears,' said Jimmy.

'What?'

'Of course she has,' said Finn.

'No, I mean on this side. There's a second ear floating above her normal one.'

'It's working!' Becky cried. 'It's actually working! Whatever you do, don't let me move.'

Lift! LIFT! All the way up and out!

Her feet ached as they tried to move, her shoulders twitched as they tried to rise up, but Jimmy and Finn didn't let them.

'No way! Y-you've got two heads,' Finn stuttered. 'That's freaky!'

It was the weirdest feeling. Becky was seeing out of two sets of eyes, one head sitting above the other.

Keep lifting! My whole body! Towards the bottle!

Her ghost head looked down and saw the rest of her ghost body lifting up out of her living one.

She was prepared for it to be painful, but it wasn't at

all – just strange. She felt her feet firmly pressed against the ground, but they were also now free and weightless, as her ghost floated next to her. She felt Jimmy and Finn pressing down on her shoulders, but her ghost was able to swing her arms about freely.

Finn looked at her, mouth wide open, head slowly shaking.

'So now you can climb the tree?' asked Jimmy.

'I don't need to,' said Becky's ghost. 'I'm a ghost, I can fly.'

Lift! she thought.

Her ghost floated up a metre above the ground.

'Wow!' cried Finn.

As Becky's ghost continued to float upwards next to the tree, she found she no longer needed to tell it to move – she was able to do it naturally.

She was a few metres up when she looked down at her living body. 'That's the top of my head!'

But she also saw the leeches – thousands of them – getting ever closer to where she, Jimmy and Finn stood on the ground.

Jimmy had noticed them too. 'Be quick, Becky!'

Becky looked up at the glow of the bottle and her ghost flew towards it, cutting through the air like a kite.

'Watch out!' called Finn.

One of the tree's branches swung straight at her. She shot to the right and the swinging branch just missed.

'Mitexi's bewitched the tree, just like she did to Lord Thistlewick!' Becky realised.

She kept a safe distance away from the tree and continued gliding up. Each branch swung out at her, but could not reach. She looked up at the glowing bottle, getting ever closer.

'Eugh! Get off!' said Finn.

With her living eyes below, Becky looked down and saw hundreds of slimy, fat leeches starting to suck onto their shoes and climb up them, searching for flesh.

'Hurry up, Becky!' Jimmy mouthed.

Becky focused all her energy on her ghost again and shot upwards. Before she knew it she was level with the top of the tree, looking right at the glowing bottle. But there was a problem – the bottle was near the tree trunk, behind several long branches.

She hovered slowly forwards. Maybe if she was extra careful, the branches wouldn't sense her. Her ghost moved over the top of one branch, careful not to touch it, and it didn't react. The bottle was within touching distance. She stretched out an arm.

SNAP! The branches swung at her. There was nothing she could do as they wrapped around her ghost and pressed her into the tree trunk just below the bottle. She didn't really feel the pain like her living body would, but far below her heart thudded in her living chest.

'Ahhh! My leg! My leg!' Jimmy cried.

Becky felt the leeches squelching up her own living leg, but she had to focus on her ghost. She squirmed, but the branches held her in a tight hug.

Her ghost eyes scanned around madly. She saw the bottle just above her. She tried to wiggle her left arm, but it was pressed firmly against the tree.

Far below, she felt dozens of tiny pricks in her legs as leeches started sucking her blood.

Becky's ghostly right arm was being held by a thinner branch. She put all her energy into that arm and forced it outwards. The branch swung away. Before it was able to grab her again, she lifted her right arm up.

Becky felt the cool touch of the bottle against her fingertips. She stretched and stretched until her hand fitted around the bottle and held it tight.

Suddenly, her ghost relaxed. All the branches let her go and moved back to their usual positions. She let herself sway there, relieved. Then she fell.

She glided down, as light as a feather, towards the ground. Her ghost body was drawn towards her living one like two magnets connecting. A tingling sensation moved through her as they met. She let out a long breath.

As her ghost hand fitted back into her living one, the bottle stopped glowing and felt a lot more solid. It was back in the living world.

'We've got the fourth bottle!'

16

The Death of Lord Thistlewick

Some people think that ghosts wear whatever they were wearing when they died. In actual fact, when ghosts die they are allowed to choose their favourite outfit to take into the ghost world with them. One man, Herbert Purple, accidentally chose his wife's swimming costume and is now stuck wearing it for all eternity. He says it is a tight fit, but he has grown to love the colour pink.

If anyone ever meets Lord Thistlewick's ghost, they are likely to see him wearing his favourite item of clothing: his treasured purple cloak.

From *My Life With Ghosts* by Eric Pockle, published after the author's death

Now Becky had the bottle, she realised the leeches had stopped attacking too, just like the tree, and were squelching slowly back towards the walls.

After a bit of searching, Finn found another door behind the tree, which led to a tunnel. Becky braced herself for another challenge, but after several twists and turns the tunnel led them back to the main entrance.

The giant rock sat there, blocking the entrance. Becky felt confident as she placed her hand on it. As she hoped, the spell Mitexi had put on the rock made it do what Becky wanted. It started to roll away from the tunnel entrance, letting them step out onto the sand.

'Fresh air!' Jimmy sighed.

'That feels good,' said Finn.

Outside in the cove it was dark. Nearby was the shimmering form of Willow, facing out to sea. As Becky stepped out onto the sand, Willow turned and her eyes shone. She soared over and hugged Becky, who couldn't help shivering from the sudden chill of the ghost.

'Sorry,' said Willow. 'I'm just so glad you made it out. What happened in there?'

'Long story,' said Finn.

'But we got the bottle. Well, Becky did,' Jimmy explained.

Becky looked over to the water. *The Caspian* was nowhere to be seen. 'Has Godiva gone already?'

Willow nodded. 'She sailed off fifteen minutes ago, shouting at her sons about what she will do to Thistlewick when she returns.'

'Then we need to get Lord Thistlewick's ghost out of these bottles.'

***

They sat around the fire again, which now showed no signs of Mitexi's fire-snake. Willow's image was the strongest Becky had ever seen it thanks to the warmth from the flames. They didn't seem to be having any effect on the bottles, though, which were all lined up next to the fire. Whatever was flickering inside each of them started to swirl, but the bottles didn't shake at all.

'It isn't enough,' said Willow. 'Lord Thistlewick is a powerful ghost. He needs even more energy.'

'What has more energy than a fire?' asked Becky.

'The sun,' said Jimmy. 'We're on the east of the island, so when it rises it will shine right onto this beach.'

'But that means we've got to wait until tomorrow. Godiva is coming back to destroy the island then!'

'And what if it's cloudy?' asked Finn.

Willow stared at the bottles. 'We'll just have to hope it isn't.'

Becky folded her arms, the confidence she had felt earlier slipping away slightly.

BANG! FIZZ!

She looked up as a bright red firework exploded far above in the night sky, starting the celebration of the end of the three hundredth Thistlewick fair.

BANG! BANG! FIZZ! Two more went off, golden and purple.

Becky thought of her mum and all the other islanders gathered together in the market square to watch the fireworks. None of them knew that tomorrow they would either meet Lord Thistlewick, or see Godiva Gibbons destroy his island.

Becky was shaken awake. She opened her eyes and it was still dark. Finn had his hand on her shoulder. He was sitting up with Jimmy.

'Where's Willow?' she asked.

'Here,' the ghost girl said, appearing next to her.

'The sunrise is about to start,' said Jimmy.

Becky just made out a thin line of light flickering across the sea towards the beach. The four bottles were lined up on the sand.

'We need to take the corks out,' said Becky.

'I've done it,' said Jimmy, holding them up to show her.

Soon, the top of the bright white sun appeared on the horizon. Light hit the bottles and shone through them, straight into Becky's face, blinding her. She squinted and shielded her eyes with a hand, but still couldn't quite see what was happening.

'Come on! Work!'

Finn stood up, also squinting. 'I'm sure one of the bottles is shaking!'

As the sun rose higher in the sky, the light on the bottles grew stronger. Becky gave up trying to see and let the white wash over her.

Smash!

'What was that?'

'Breaking glass,' said Jimmy, who had turned away to shield his eyes.

Smash! Smash!

'The bottles! It has to be. Can you see anything, Willow?'

Smash!

'No, but I can sense a great amount of power.'

Becky reached into her pocket for the EMF detector. Before she brought it out, the whiteness started to change colour. Becky's vision was filled with purple. She closed her eyes but the colour seemed to be burnt into them.

When she opened them again, the shape of a person was there in front of her, but light was shining through him – through the purple cloak that billowed around him.

'Lord Thistlewick?' she mouthed.

'Hello, Becky Evans,' a deep voice replied.

***

They all sat there, speechless, as the sun rose up past the ghost, letting them see him clearly.

He was even taller than Becky had imagined from the paintings, but he looked just as grand. There was no beard on his face, which was strong and square, and his eyes and mouth seemed to be carved with kindness. Lord Thistlewick didn't have a silver or a green glow around him, like the other ghosts Becky had seen – his glow was golden.

She couldn't believe it as he floated over, flicked his purple cloak from under him and sat down beside them.

Willow dared to speak first. 'It-it is a great honour to meet you, Lord Thistlewick.'

He bowed his head and smiled at her.

'You … you know my name,' Becky stuttered.

Lord Thistlewick fixed two dark eyes on her. 'Of course. And Jimmy Cole, Finn Gailsborough and Willow Summercroft. The four people who have put such great effort into bringing my ghost back. I have followed your adventures from within the bottles.' He stretched out his arms, each like a tree trunk. 'I must say, it is a relief to be out. Rather cramped inside.'

Becky stared at Lord Thistlewick, trying to keep her mouth from falling open. There were so many questions she wanted to ask him.

Finn thought of one before her. 'Lord Thistlewick, we've been using your near-death experiences to find the bottles, but no one knows how you actually died. We know you set out in *The Caspian* on an adventure, but then you went missing. So, how did you die?'

'Finn!' said Becky, thinking it was a bit rude to ask.

Jimmy was frowning too.

Lord Thistlewick only smiled. 'It is a good question, and one I have been waiting a long time to answer.'

How Lord Thistlewick *actually* died

(according to Lord Thistlewick)

Everyone on the island thought I was setting off on an adventure on that fateful day in **1723**.

I was, in fact, travelling to England to confront Grinlin Gibbons.

In **1717**, the horse my son was riding was poinoned. The horse collapsed and my son fell and died. A man called Walter Anion was found guilty of the crime and sent to prison.

At the time, I was too caught up in my grief to realise who the real criminal was. Years later, evidence was brought to me that revealed the truth: Grinlin Gibbons had poisoned the horse. The man I had let marry my daughter, Coral-Anne! It was all part of Gibbons's plan to gain my trust and take my money.

I travelled in secret to Manglehorn Manor, where Coral-Anne and Gibbons lived. Coral-Anne was away, so I accused the man of his crimes. He, of course, denied them. Claiming to be deeply insulted, he challenged me to a duel. I accepted, as any gentleman has to.

'On the count of three, gentlemen,' said Gibbons's manservant.

We aimed our guns at each other. I was a quick and expert shot, but I had no desire to kill him. I would disarm Gibbons before he got his shot in...

'Three.'

... Then I could make him confess to his crimes. From metres away, I could still see the evil in his eyes.

'Two.'

BANG!

A cold sensation rushed through me. I had been shot in the heart.

'My gun! I did not mean... It just went off early. Lord Thistlewick, are you...?' I heard Gibbons's sly voice acting concerned.

My vision went black. As I slipped from life to death, I heard him striding up to me.

He whispered in my ear, 'I did poison your son's horse. And now I have killed you, your money is mine.'

Becky shook her head. 'Grinlin Gibbons really was evil. Does anyone else know?'

'No one. Very soon after my murder, as a ghost, I realised I had to go into hiding.'

'Why?' asked Jimmy.

'Gibbons had covered up my murder, telling people my boat had sunk on my last adventure. He was expecting to inherit all my worldly treasures in my will, but I destroyed it,' Lord Thistlewick explained. 'Before

I sailed to confront him, I hid my treasure on my island and did not tell a soul about it. I also had to hide my ghost, so that Gibbons could not find me and force me to reveal the treasure's location.'

'And Mitexi helped you do it,' said Becky.

'She did. Mitexi, it turned out, was my closest ally.'

'But why did you split your ghost between four bottles?' asked Willow. 'It must have been so painful.'

'It certainly was, but by getting Mitexi to hide the bottles, I knew it would stop Gibbons. He was too greedy and lazy to put that much effort in. Only good people willing to go through the challenges I had faced myself would find me. And here I am looking at the four of you now.' He smiled at each of them in turn. 'But you must have had a good reason for your efforts. Why did you bring my ghost back?'

17

Three Hundred Letters

I was France's foremost fashion designer. I regularly worked for royalty and some of the world's greatest celebrities. Lord Thistlewick's reputation was immense. When he asked me to design his official family emblem, I was greatly honoured.

I came up with many complex and beautiful ideas for the emblem, but Lord Thistlewick preferred my simplest design: a candle to represent the 'wick' in his name, sitting in the middle of two thistle leaves.

An extract from *Ma Vie en Mode*, the autobiography of Rosalie Bertin (translated from the French)

'Grinlin Gibbons's descendant, Godiva Gibbons, also wants to take your treasure. She's been blackmailing us,' Becky explained. 'Godiva told me that if I don't find your treasure and give it to her, she will destroy every building on Thistlewick until she finds it herself.'

'I see,' said Lord Thistlewick, his voice deep, his face

deadly serious for a second. 'But that is not why you found my ghost, is it?'

'No. We found you because you outrank Godiva, so you can stop her destroying the island.'

Lord Thistlewick stroked his chin. 'When is she planning her "attack"?'

'Later today,' said Finn.

'It seems that Godiva Gibbons is cut from the same cloth as Grinlin. I most certainly will not allow her to destroy my island.' Lord Thistlewick stood up, his ghost towering over them. 'But nor will I allow her to take my treasure. You have all been very brave thus far. Your bravery will need to continue over the next few hours.'

'Do … do you have a plan?' asked Becky.

'I do indeed, Becky, and it will involve everyone on Thistlewick.'

Becky felt a tingle of excitement race around her body. Her idea was working! Lord Thistlewick was going to stop Godiva.

'This is what you must do,' Lord Thistlewick continued. 'Bring them all together. Get everyone on the island to light a candle outside their houses before Godiva Gibbons arrives today.'

'How should we do that?'

Lord Thistlewick smiled at her. 'You are the first people to have ever found my ghost, so I am sure you will think of something.'

He moved over to Willow, bent down and whispered to her. She nodded, smiled at Becky, then disappeared.

'Wait!' Becky cried. 'Lord Thistlewick…'

But the ghost was moving away from them.

He looked back. 'I have confidence in you, Becky Evans. I will return when you need me.'

Lord Thistlewick's cloak seemed to catch a breeze. It swept around him and in a flash of purple he was gone.

Becky turned to her two living friends. 'That definitely just happened, didn't it? We just met Lord Thistlewick?'

Finn and Jimmy nodded, eyes wide.

'But how can we get everyone on Thistlewick to light a candle outside their houses before Godiva comes back?' she asked.

Jimmy looked down and started turning the corks from the bottles around in his hand.

'Your mum's the postmistress, Becky. You could send everyone letters,' Finn suggested.

'But why would they listen to us? Why would they light a candle because we tell them to?'

'They might if the letters have Lord Thistlewick's official emblem on them,' said Jimmy.

He held one of the corks out to Becky, then turned it around – on the bottom was an image of a candle in between two thistle leaves.

'Only Lord Thistlewick used this emblem. He used it to seal his official letters in wax.'

'Jimmy, you're a genius!' cried Becky. 'But do you think he will mind us using it now?'

'I think it's what he wants. If people get letters with this stamped on them, they'll realise that Lord Thistlewick really has returned, and that he wants them to light a candle.'

***

Lord Thistlewick has returned! He requests that you light a candle outside your house at

Becky copied this message out onto another piece of paper and added it to the pile. There were over three hundred houses on Thistlewick – it was a good job Mum had an endless supply of paper and envelopes in the post office back room.

Jimmy came in with a boxful of candles. 'This is every candle I could find in my house and yours.'

'We'll need more than that if we're giving every house a candle.'

'We're not giving these away,' said Jimmy. 'Everyone will have their own candles – there's enough power cuts on the island to guarantee that. We can melt these ones and use the wax to seal the letters with Lord Thistlewick's official emblem.'

The post office door jangled open and Finn appeared.

'Is Mum still packing things away out there?' asked Becky.

'Yep, the square's in chaos at the moment with all the stalls coming down.' Finn sat down next to her. 'Granddad says the boats are coming to collect the fair equipment at five o'clock.'

'OK, I'll tell everyone to light a candle at quarter to five. How long do we have until then?'

'Two hours,' said Jimmy.

'Two hours to finish and post over three hundred letters. We'd better hurry up!' said Becky.

She added '4.45 tonight' to one of the pieces of paper and signed her name under it. She handed the letter to Jimmy. He folded it up, then took out a matchbox and lit a candle. He held the candle over the letter until the wax dripped onto it, forming a circle. Jimmy then took the cork from Lord Thistlewick's bottle and stamped it onto the wax. As he removed the cork, Lord Thistlewick's official emblem appeared in the wax.

Becky finished another letter and handed it to him. Finn grabbed some candles and a cork from one of the other bottles, and helped Jimmy to stamp the letters.

'This is definitely going to work, isn't it?' asked Finn.

'Don't know,' said Becky. 'We'll find out in two hours' time. But Lord Thistlewick has a plan and I trust him.'

18

Attack!

Of all the machines used in the demolition of buildings, wrecking balls are the most powerful and destructive.

An extract from *Demolition for Dummies* by Archie Rawgabbit

Becky tapped her fingers nervously and watched the clock hands on top of the post office move to 4.46. Still no one had come out to light a candle.

'It's not working! We've got to think of a new plan,' she told Jimmy and Finn.

'Let's knock on people's doors,' suggested Finn.

'There's only fourteen minutes until Godiva arrives,' said Jimmy. 'We don't have time.'

A door flung open nearby and Mr Finch came out. He saw the children and darted over to them.

'I can't find a candle anywhere. Lord Thistlewick is coming! He wants me to light a candle! Do you have any?'

Before Becky could reply, Mr Morris called from across the square, 'Have one of mine, Mr Finch, and hurry. Lord Thistlewick could be here any moment!'

Soon, other doors opened around the square and people busied themselves with lighting candles and placing them on their doorsteps.

Becky, Jimmy and Finn looked at each other and nodded confidently – it was working!

Mum walked out of the post office behind Becky. She waved the letter in front of her. 'I have just opened this. Why is it in your handwriting, and on post office paper?'

'Light a candle and you'll see.' Becky held one out, hoping Mum wouldn't kick up a fuss.

'What are you up to, Becky Evans?' Mum looked around the square at everyone else doing what the letter said, sighed, and took the candle.

Becky let herself smile. Whatever Lord Thistlewick had planned with these candles, they would be ready.

Everyone stood by their front doors, candles burning bright on the doorsteps. Some looked up to the sky, as if expecting Lord Thistlewick to descend through a cloud.

The post office clock chimed five. Becky gulped – Godiva would be arriving at the Thistlewick harbour with her boats and machines.

'When will Lord Thistlewick arrive?' Mr Morris shouted across the square.

'She's the true Thistlewickian.' Mr Finch pointed at Becky. 'She should know what's happening.'

'My daughter is not the true Thistlewickian, whatever that may be,' Mum said, glaring.

Mr Finch ignored her. 'Well, Becky?'

'I … I don't know,' she admitted, trying not to worry. Surely Lord Thistlewick would reveal what he had planned before Godiva showed up. 'We have to trust Lord Thistlewick and wait.'

A low rumbling started then. Becky felt the ground shaking under her.

'Is it him?' asked Mr Finch.

'It's a monster!' cried Mr Morris from his house in the furthest corner of the square.

Becky turned and saw a huge machine next him. A long metal crane extended upwards, shining yellow, with a giant black ball hanging from it – a wrecking ball.

'It's Godiva,' Finn mouthed beside Becky.

Becky made out the woman sitting behind the controls of the machine, every bit as round as the ball hanging from it.

'Your time is up, Becky Evans!' Godiva called down, her voice sharp. 'Did you find Lord Thistlewick's ghost?'

'Yes, I did,' Becky replied, trying to sound confident.

Gasps echoed around the square and lots of people whispered about her *really* being the true Thistlewickian.

But Godiva's voice cut through them. 'And have you got his treasure for me?'

'No.'

'Then hand him over and I will make him tell me where he's been hiding it!'

'I can't do that,' Becky called back, her body tensing as she tried to control her nerves.

'You know what will happen if you don't. I will destroy every building on this island until I have found Lord Thistlewick's treasure, starting with the post office.'

The machine rumbled and the wrecking ball started to swing ominously.

Mum stepped forwards. 'Are you crazy? You can't do that!'

'I am Godiva Gibbons, Lord Thistlewick's descendant. I can do what I want.'

Becky looked around desperately. Where was Lord Thistlewick? As soon as he showed up, he could outrank Godiva and stop her.

'We won't let you!' yelled Mr Finch.

He moved away from his front door and stood in front of the wrecking ball. Several others joined him, forming a line to block the machine from entering the square.

Becky just made out Godiva rolling her eyes. 'I thought this might happen, so I brought reinforcements.'

From around the machine, a large circus cage appeared, being wheeled by Bartley and Barney. Behind the bars, Becky recognised the man in bright Hawaiian shirt and shorts.

'Spooky Steve!'

'I'm sorry, Becky,' he said, voice shaking. 'Godiva

made me do it. She threatened to have my TV show cancelled if I didn't.'

'What did she make you do?' asked Becky.

Steve bit his lip and turned away.

'Steve has called up a few friends to help me,' said Godiva.

A green glow flickered around the wrecking ball.

Out of nowhere a swarm of ghosts surrounded the machine. Ghosts of pirates, all waving swords and jeering. Ghosts of prisoners in balls and chains. Many of the creepy shadow-ghosts from the forest. Becky even saw several swirling black masses that must be spectres.

'All the evil ghosts of Thistlewick,' Becky realised.

Mr Finch and the other living people backed away as the ghosts started hissing, '*Dead! Dead! Dead!*'

Becky stared back at Godiva, whose smile was as wide as the ones painted on the clowns. She had hundreds of ghosts on her side, their green glow filling the square, their chants and cheers ringing around it.

How was there any chance of saving Thistlewick now, even if Lord Thistlewick did show up?

'Don't worry, Becky,' said Willow, appearing beside her.

'Willow! Where did you go? Where's Lord Thistle-wick?'

'He will be here when you need him.'

'We need him now!'

'Well, for now you have all of us.'

'Us?'

Willow pointed around the market. On every door-step, next to each of the burning candles, more ghosts appeared, but glowing silver. Good ghosts. By the post office candle, several men floated, wearing blue post office outfits similar to Mum's.

'Hello, Barbara,' one of them said. 'I am Enoch Inverkip, postmaster until 1855. May I just say that you are doing a marvellous job with the post office.'

'Um … thank you!' Mum replied, eyebrows rising in bafflement.

Mr Finch, Mr Morris and the other people in the market were looking around, speechless.

'What on earth?' cried Godiva.

'We have all come together, Becky,' Willow explained. 'The good ghosts of Thistlewick agreed to enter the living world. All we needed was the power from the candles.'

The rumbling sound returned, but this time it didn't come from Godiva's machine. Many more living people and ghosts appeared, piling in through every entrance, filling the market.

Becky saw Mrs Didsbury waving a rolling pin and Albert, brandishing an oar, with several ghostly fishermen behind him.

As Becky looked around, the silver glow of the good

ghosts now filled her vision more than the sickly green of the evil ghosts.

'Hundreds of living people and thousands of ghosts are here, all ready to defend Thistlewick,' said Willow.

Becky glanced back at Godiva. Now it was the woman who looked worried, and Becky who smiled.

Godiva screwed up her face. Her whole body shook. With an ear-splitting scream she yelled, 'Attack!'

19

The Battle for Thistlewick Island

Those ghosts you can count as good generally have a silver glow around them. Ghosts of a more evil persuasion usually have a green glow. Why this is, I do not know. It is one mystery I have never been able to solve.

From *My Life With Ghosts* by Eric Pockle,
published after the author's death

The ghost pirates, criminals and shadow-ghosts charged forwards, shouting, *'Dead! Dead! Dead!'*

Becky wondered if there was anyone in charge of the good ghosts, like Godiva was ordering the evil ones. As one, Willow and the others floated forwards to face their enemy.

'Dead! Dead! Dead!'

The good ghosts stood firm, a wall of silver, as the attacking force entered the square.

Finn was the first living person the make a move. 'We have to help!'

He turned and ran through the sea of ghosts, straight for Godiva's machine, yelling, 'Yaaahhhhh!'

'Bartley! Barney! Get him!' Becky heard Godiva call.

The clowns stepped in front of the machine and grabbed Finn easily. Becky saw him kick and flail his arms as they started dragging him away.

She ran after them, only to be pushed back as Mr Finch stumbled past, fending off a scar-covered ghost pirate with a saw. Although the pirate was a ghost, his sword was real enough and there was a *clang* as it hit the saw.

Becky noticed none of the good ghosts had weapons and even the evil pirate-ghosts weren't using their swords against the good ghosts. Instead they were all trying to grab hold of each other. Becky guessed that between ghosts a fight meant trying to take as much energy away from your opponent as possible.

'Get them! Get them all!' Godiva cried.

'Dead! Dead! Dead!'

The images of several of the silver ghosts nearest to Becky flickered weakly, including Willow, who was caught in a headlock by a shadow-ghost. Looking around the square, Becky could now see more of a green glow than silver, which she guessed meant that Godiva's army was winning. Where was Lord Thistlewick? They needed him!

'Finn's right, we have to do something,' Becky told Jimmy. 'Get the living people to help the ghosts.'

'How?'

Becky thought quickly. 'Salt and cold, that's what we need. You need to pour salt around the edge of the square. Good ghosts can get past salt, but evil ones can't. It'll trap them inside.'

Jimmy nodded. He ducked under a pirate's sword and headed off left to pass on the message.

'Mum!' said Becky. 'We need cold stuff. Water, fans, anything like that. Ghosts hate the cold – it takes their energy away.'

Mum's mouth hung open, looking from the fighting ghosts to her daughter. Then a determined look fired up in her eyes. 'I'll get some fans from the post office. There's a hose on the other side of the square we could use.'

Mum disappeared into the post office. Becky started to creep along the edge of the market square, trying to avoid being seen by Godiva as she made for the hose.

'The girl! Stop Becky Evans, whatever she is doing!' came Godiva's cry. 'Bring her to me!'

Becky gritted her teeth, but the ghosts around her didn't seem to hear the order. They were too busy fighting.

'*Dead! Dead! Dead!*'

She crept past Albert fending off a ghost's axe with his oar.

Then a deep wail filled Becky's ears. She recognised it instantly. She looked up at the black spectre hovering above her. It formed itself into a ball, crackling with electric energy.

Becky dived sideways as it fired its tentacles at her. She knocked into Mr Finch and they both fell to the ground. The pirate he had been fighting leered over them and raised his sword to strike. The spectre, trying to reach Becky, shot straight into the ghost.

'Aaarrrggghhh!' the ghost screamed, and he started attacking the spectre.

'Mr Finch, can you get … the hose over there and … fire water at Godiva's ghosts,' said Becky in between breaths.

He nodded and got up. Becky spied a thin gap between the butcher's shop and the baker's and crawled into it.

From there, she could see most of the battle. Finn was to her right, still trying fight off the clowns so he could reach the wrecking ball machine.

Above them, Godiva sat inside the machine. She was looking frantically around the square. 'Where has the girl gone? What is she up to? Find her! Find Becky Evans!'

Becky pressed herself into the darkness between the buildings.

She could just make out Jimmy far to the left with Mr Morris, carrying large bags Becky guessed were full of salt. Mum was passing fans around. The rest of the square was a mess of living people and ghosts, and hovering above them all were three spectres.

Like vultures, each spectre was firing its tentacles randomly down at whoever was below, sucking away their energy and growing bigger and bigger.

Mr Finch had made it to the hose and started to shoot jets of cold water around the market square. It didn't seem to be working, though. The water was hitting both evil and good ghosts. They fled away from it, but carried on fighting once they were out of the hose's firing line.

'I've had enough of this! My treasure must be under one of these buildings. Time to knock down the post office!' yelled Godiva.

Over the screams and yells of fighting, Becky heard the rumble of the wrecking ball machine starting up.

'Becky!' Willow appeared in the darkness beside her, her image flickering wildly. 'What are you going to do?'

'If Lord Thistlewick isn't coming, then I have to stop Godiva myself,' said Becky. 'All her ghosts want to do is have a big fight. She's the only one focused on her plan. If I stop her, then I stop her plan.'

'But how are you going to do that?'

***

Becky looked up as Godiva started to move the machine forwards.

'Wait!' someone called.

The machine juddered to a halt.

'What is it?' Godiva peered out. 'You!'

Becky stood right in front of it, centimetres away from the giant wrecking ball.

'Get out of my way! I've got a post office to destroy.'

'No!' Becky called back.

'Bartley! Barney! Get her away from my machine!'

The two clowns broke off from fighting Finn and went for Becky.

Finn grabbed at their green and orange wigs, but they didn't come off – the clowns' whole bodies went flying backwards. Becky laughed – they weren't wearing wigs: it was their actual hair!

'Ghosts, get the girl out of my way!' Godiva tried.

But the ghosts were too caught up fighting each other to notice.

'Fine, I'll do it myself!' Godiva muttered. 'Girl, I'm warning you, stand there any longer and I'll knock you over.'

Becky stayed exactly where she was, staring up at Godiva.

Godiva puffed out her cheeks. 'You can't say I didn't warn you!'

She flicked a switch on the machine and the crane lifted up the wrecking ball – almost as big as Becky and a thousand times heavier. It started to swing back.

But Becky didn't move.

'Becky!' she heard Finn cry as the ball shot forwards.

It was coming straight for her, but she stood her ground. At the point the ball should have hit her, it didn't. It passed straight through.

'What the—' Godiva spat, standing up and staring out of the machine.

Becky's ghost grinned. She had distracted Godiva just long enough. She watched as her living body appeared behind Godiva on the machine.

Godiva was still looking down in disbelief at the ghost of Becky, while Becky's living body reached around Godiva and plucked the key from the machine's ignition. The engine stopped rumbling and the wrecking ball came to a stop.

'Boo!' said Becky's living body.

Godiva swung around. 'How did you… You little—'

She tried to grab her, but Becky leapt from the machine.

She landed next to her ghost and they joined together again. Becky took a deep breath – it had worked!

There was a flash of orange hair as Barney dived at her.

'Finn! Catch!' Becky threw him the key.

He did, but Bartley jumped at Finn.

Jimmy was nearby, pouring salt along the ground.

'Jimmy, catch!' Finn lobbed the key at him.

It landed in Jimmy's hand and he threw it back to Becky.

She threw it to Finn. He threw it to Jimmy, and the clowns didn't know where to turn.

Jimmy was about to throw to Becky again, but stopped.

'Hurry up, Jimmy,' Becky told him, not understanding why he had suddenly frozen. 'I'm going to take the key and chuck it in the sea.'

His eyes widened just as Becky felt something sharp pressing into her neck.

'Give me the key, boy, or you don't want to know what will happen to Becky Evans,' Godiva hissed.

20

The True Thistlewickian(s)

> When the rock on Watcher's Cliff
> falls again, Lord Thistlewick will
> return and a true Thistlewickian
> will find his treasure...

Mitexi Shelldrake's prophecy

The sight of Becky held at sword-point by Godiva Gibbons made many people around the square freeze. A strange silence fell.

'Get away from my daughter!' Mum yelled, running towards her.

'No, Mum, don't.' Becky's heart was pounding, but she tried to keep her voice steady. She had realised what Mitexi's prophecy meant. 'Even with the key – even if you knock down every building – you won't find Lord Thistlewick's treasure, Godiva.'

'Why?'

'Because you aren't a true Thistlewickian.'

'If I'm not, then who possibly could be? You think it's Steve? Ha! He doesn't have the guts.'

'No, *I'm* a true Thistlewickian,' said Becky. She felt the sword press into her neck.

'I knew it!' Mrs Didsbury whispered to a nearby ghost, loud enough for Becky to hear.

She looked at her. 'But so are you, Mrs Didsbury, and everyone else who is fighting to save Thistlewick. All the good people here make this island what it is.'

'And what is that?' Godiva sounded like she'd had enough of talking. If she pressed the sword any further, Becky was worried she would soon end up headless in the ghost world.

'A community!' said Mayor Merryweather.

'Yes!' cried several others.

'Where everyone cares about everyone else,' said Mr Morris.

'We all look out for each other,' added Albert.

'It has always been that way, right from the day Lord Thistlewick created this island,' said a ghost wearing an ancient-looking cloak.

'Ha! What utter nonsense. Give me the k … the k … the k—' But Godiva couldn't finish her sentence.

A shimmering gold beam had appeared in front of them – a glow far brighter than the silver and green of the ghosts. She dropped her sword.

Becky ran to join Jimmy and Finn as the golden glow grew until it was the shape of a large person. The ghosts gasped, staring at it.

Lord Thistlewick's head appeared in the light first, his golden mane of hair shining brightly.

'Is it him? Has he come back?' people whispered.

In a rush of wind, Lord Thistlewick's purple cloak materialised, swishing around his body, surrounding him in purple.

The crowd of islanders and all the good ghosts broke into a cheer.

Ginger-Anne Curly was wide-eyed with shock. 'He … he doesn't have a beard!' And with that, she fainted.

'Well, well, Lord Thistlewick. It is good of you to finally show up,' said Godiva, her hands twitching, her lips curling into a snarl. 'You don't want to see your precious island destroyed, do you?'

'I do not,' he replied, his voice deep.

'Then you will tell me where to find your treasure.'

'You will never get my treasure, Godiva, for the same reason your ancestor Grinlin never did.'

'Why is that?!' Godiva screeched.

'For the reason these people have just told you. Grinlin, like you, did not realise that my real treasure isn't gold or diamonds or riches.'

Becky frowned – what did Lord Thistlewick mean?

'My real treasure is my island and the community of people on it. That is something you cannot put a price on, and something only a true Thistlewickian would understand.'

He looked at Becky as he said this, and she was sure he winked.

'So there's nothing?' Godiva spat. 'I've wasted my time for nothing!'

Lord Thistlewick raised an eyebrow and continued, looking around the crowd. 'Now, all you ghosts working for Godiva, listen to me. My ghost was split between four bottles, in which I stayed for nearly three hundred years. Can you imagine how painful that was? Worse than death, believe me. This is my island and if you wish to stay here, I can happily arrange for you all to be split between your own bottles. I am not afraid to be generous. Let us say, oh, a hundred bottles each. How does that sound?'

The various pirates and criminals and shadow-ghosts looked at each other. They dropped their weapons, which all clinked and clanked on the ground.

'No, I didn't think so. Then please leave my island and never return!' boomed Lord Thistlewick.

The ghosts started to flee, their green glows shooting left and right, fighting each other to be the first to leave the market. But they couldn't get out, because it was now surrounded by salt.

'Upwards, lads!' came a gruff cry from a pirate.

As one, Becky watched them soar into the air, creating a shining green line, like a lightning bolt in reverse.

'Stop them, Steve!' cried Godiva.

But from within the cage he shook his head, and

joined in as everyone left in the market cheered again. Everyone except for Godiva and her clowns, who were both doing their best to cower behind the wrecking ball.

'As for you, Godiva,' said Lord Thistlewick, puffing out his chest. 'It isn't too late. Why don't you give up your greed and join us here on Thistlewick Island? Learn what it is to be a true Thistlewickian.'

Becky stepped forwards and said, 'I don't want to fight you, Godiva. I'll even forgive you for threatening to knock down the post office.'

Godiva glared at Becky for several seconds, then her blazing eyes turned on Lord Thistlewick.

'Grinlin Gibbons was right to get rid of you,' she spat. 'Boys, get Steve's cage. We're leaving.'

'Actually, I … I'd like to stay,' said Steve quietly.

Lord Thistlewick smiled at him and clicked his fingers. The cage door fell open. Steve stepped out and went to join Becky. He held out his hand and she shook it.

Godiva's face was like a red balloon about to be popped.

'AAARRRGGGHHH!' She turned around and stomped out of the market square, the two clowns scampering after her.

Everyone else was silent for a while.

'We did it,' Becky said under her breath.

'Yes, Becky, you did,' said Lord Thistlewick, beaming

at her. 'Three cheers for Becky, Jimmy, Finn and Willow. Hip hip!'

'Hooray!' all the people, living and dead, cheered.

'Hip hip!'

'Hooray!'

'Hip hip!'

'Hooray!'

Becky felt a smile spreading over her face as she looked around at them all.

She saw that the noise of the cheering had woken Ginger-Ann Curly. Lord Thistlewick floated over to her and held out a hand to help her up.

At the sight of this, Ginger-Ann went cross eyed and fainted once more.

Lord Thistlewick's Treasure

'I have always believed that Lord Thistlewick had a beard. All I have ever needed is the proof, and now I have it!

'Lord Thistlewick himself (well, his ghost) told me that when he was a young man he grew a French Fork. It is a type of beard I was not familiar with, so I asked him to draw it for me.

'Here, I am proud to present Lord Thistlewick's very own sketch of his very own beard. It was strawberry blonde in colour, apparently.'

Ginger-Ann Curly, president of the Thistlewick Beard Appreciation Society

From *Beard Monthly* magazine, this year's September edition

A party started almost straight away and was still going strong by the time it had got dark. Everyone kept the candles lit outside their houses and most of the good ghosts stayed to join in the celebration.

One ghost who hadn't stayed was Lord Thistlewick himself. Once he had helped lift Ginger-Ann off the ground, and shaken hands with Albert, he had simply disappeared into thin air. This left some people wondering whether they really had seen him, or just imagined it all. Mrs Didsbury had asked Becky if she knew where he was, but she didn't have a clue.

After that, many people had gathered around Becky, asking her to tell them the story about how she found Lord Thistlewick's bottles. She must have repeated it all twenty times or more.

Now she was dancing in a circle with Jimmy, Finn and Willow, as a ghost band played. None of them could stop grinning.

Behind her happiness, though, Becky wondered whether she would ever see Lord Thistlewick again.

When the music died down, people both living and dead sat around on blankets chatting. Jimmy and Finn were deep in conversation with Willow, asking what her teachers had been like.

Becky left them to it and slipped away from the party. She didn't want to answer any more questions and needed to be alone for a bit.

She decided to head to Watcher's Cliff, where her adventure had started with the rock falling three days before. She stood there and looked out to sea.

'Three hundred years ago today I took my first step

onto this island,' a deep voice said next to her. 'This was always my favourite view from it.'

She turned and smiled. 'Lord Thistlewick. We've been having a party. Why did you leave?'

'I saw that Thistlewick Island is in good hands,' he replied, returning her smile. 'So I went to see Mitexi in the forest, to thank her for her help before she leaves.'

'Before she leaves?'

'Ghosts only exist while they have a purpose, Becky. Mitexi's was to make sure the right person found my bottles, and she did just that. Now that she has fulfilled her purpose, she no longer needs to be a ghost.'

Becky nodded slowly. She understood.

'And I must also thank you,' said Lord Thistlewick. 'I was there for the whole fight, but I kept myself invisible and watched everything you did.'

'Why didn't you show yourself sooner?'

'You were doing fine without me. You should be very proud.'

'Thank you,' said Becky, and she realised that she was proud – not just of herself, but of everyone who had helped.

They stood and watched the waves gently lapping onto the beach below.

After a while, Lord Thistlewick leaned closer. 'I bet you were a little disappointed when I said that my real treasure wasn't gold and diamonds.'

Becky hesitated, unsure what to say.

'It is OK to admit it, Becky. We all love a bit of gold, me especially.' He ran his fingers over the gleaming buttons of his cloak.

'I suppose I was a bit disappointed,' she said quietly.

Lord Thistlewick nodded. 'Then I have something to show you.'

He swished his purple cloak out and Becky suddenly found herself wrapped inside it.

'Hold on tight,' said Lord Thistlewick.

She felt herself being lifted off the ground, but, as she rose, she saw her body still there below. Lord Thistlewick had somehow lifted her ghost up out of it.

They soared up into the sky, air rushing through Becky's hair, until they were high above Thistlewick. Looking down, she could just make out her body, a small speck on the edge of the cliff.

'Wow!' Becky felt breathless, but at the same time perfectly safe inside the cloak. 'It's beautiful, even at night.'

It was amazing seeing the shape of the whole island, carved into the sea. The lights from the candles shone brightly, little dots far below. This was Thistlewick Island. Her home.

'I meant it when I said this island is my real treasure,' said Lord Thistlewick. 'But there is plenty of gold too, and it is hidden on the island. Can you see where?'

Becky frowned. 'No.'

'Follow the light, Becky.'

She looked closely at the candlelight. The candles all formed lines, like a giant dot-to-dot drawing. She realised that each and every line was pointing to the same spot on Thistlewick, a patch of ground behind the post office.

Becky held her finger towards it.

'You are correct,' said Lord Thistlewick.

'All through the battle the gold was only a few metres away from Godiva?'

'Yes.' Lord Thistlewick chuckled. 'It wasn't meant for her, though. It is there for the time when Thistlewick Island needs it most.'

'When will that be?' asked Becky.

'You are a true Thistlewickian, Becky. You will know.'

A seagull flew past them. As it caught sight of the two people floating in mid-air it squawked madly, stopped flapping its wings and plummeted down through the air.

'Oh dear, I seem to be having that sort of effect today. I think it is time I return you to your friends, Becky,' said Lord Thistlewick.

They flew back down towards the island. Becky felt like a bird coming into land, the ground steadily sweeping closer. In no time at all she was back in her living body and felt solid rock under her feet again.

She walked back across the island, Lord Thistlewick floating along beside her. They didn't say anything – Becky didn't feel like she needed to.

'Becky!' Willow came up to her when she arrived back at the square. 'Where did you get to?'

Becky turned to say thank you to Lord Thistlewick, but there was only darkness where he had been.

'Oh, Lord Thistlewick's gone.'

Willow nodded.

Becky had a strange feeling he hadn't just made himself invisible this time. 'Can you see him in the ghost world?'

'No,' the ghost girl replied.

Becky thought about what Lord Thistlewick had said about ghosts and purposes. 'Do you think he has fulfilled his purpose?'

Willow considered this for a moment. 'Lord Thistlewick wanted to make sure there was someone here to look after his island. You have shown him that there are lots of people who will. So yes, I think he has.'

Becky looked around all the gathered people – the true Thistlewickians, both living and dead – and smiled.

The ghost band struck up their music again, playing a lively tune on trumpets and trombones. Willow and Becky went back over to Jimmy and Finn. Becky grabbed their hands and led them outside the square, to the place just behind the post office where she now knew Lord Thistlewick's treasure was buried.

Together, on that spot, they danced long into the night.

Read Becky's other adventures:

When the world-famous ghost hunter, Spooky Steve, investigates Becky's home above the post office, the ghost of Walter Anion appears and curses the place. Can Becky figure out how to stop this curse, before everything she knows and loves is destroyed forever?

Becky gets trapped inside the abandoned Thicket House by a monsterous ghost, known as 'the spectre'. As the spectre's evil plans become clear, she has to battle her fears and fight for her life. Can she escape from Thicket House before it's too late?

www.luketemple.co.uk

Luke's 'Felix Dashwood' series

30 ghost pirates
20 hypnotised kids
10 creepy rag toys
3 evil head teachers
2 shipwrecks
and **1** brave main character: Felix!

Find out more at:

www.luketemple.co.uk